SOLSTICE

―――――――――――

BY

JACK FRERKER

To the Dunns, with love!
Fr. Jack

PAX PUBLICATIONS — OLYMPIA, WASHINGTON

Published by PAX Publications
7710 56th Avenue NE, Olympia WA 98516
www.paxpublications.com

Copyright © 2004 by Jack Frerker. All rights reserved. Save for short quotes or citations for purposes of literary critique or review, no part of this book may be reproduced, stored in a retrieval system or transmitted – in any form or by any means, electronic, mechanical, photocopying, recording or otherwise – without the author's express written permission.

Printed in the U S A, by Bang Printing of Brainerd MN

This is a work of fiction – all names, characters and incidents are from the author's imagination or used fictitiously. Reference to real persons is not intended nor should be inferred.

LIBRARY OF CONGRESS CATALOGING-IN-PUBLICATION DATA

Frerker, Jack, 1937-
    SOLSTICE
    ISBN 0-9740080-1-X

Also from Pax Publications by Jack Frerker:
HEAT (ISBN 0-9740080-0-1 – $13.00)

ACKNOWLEDGMENTS

To Paula Buckner, for editorial suggestions and proofreading assistance, and to Garn Turner for another lovely cover, my deep gratitude. And thanks to Richard Swanson, my webmaster and technical wizard, for again turning my words into printable copy. I'm also grateful to Father Robert Darow, my classmate, friend and actual current pastor of St. Hilary's, for serving as my Chicago-land guru.

Thanks also to Barry Halgrimson, whose insistent encouragement and offer of a Rocky Mountain retreat in which to begin my writer's journey many years ago first got my fiction onto paper. And my gratitude, as well, to Don and Elaine Petersen, who similarly gave me space in their Florida home several years later to continue work on that first book, which I hope to put into print soon.

Many friends have come to believe in my unlikely sleuth, and through their encouragement, growing numbers of others are also coming to know and enjoy him and his world. That world, one of my own invention, continues to feed my imagination, as I hope it does yours. Thank you for your willingness to peek into it.

Jack Frerker

CHAPTER I – NORTHWARD

Father John Henry Wintermann found himself leaving his beloved Southern Illinois. He was on I-55 heading to Chicago. It wasn't his first drive to the big city, but it was, oddly enough, his first solo trip. And of all times, it was in mid-December – Saturday, the sixteenth, to be exact. Not exactly his first choice for things to do right before Christmas.

He recalled the conversation that prompted the trip.

"Father?"

"Yes."

"Kathleen Schmitz. Got a moment to talk?"

"Sure. What's up?"

"I found out a few minutes ago that Mom just died in Chicago."

"I'm so sorry, Kath. What happened?"

"Oh, Father, she'd been ill with cancer, and my two sisters had been taking care of her for some months now. The cancer had been progressing slowly, but all of a sudden this week it went on a rampage and took her quicker than ever we expected."

"Are you all right?"

"Yes, and my sisters too. We just talked. Mom wants to be buried in Chicago. You may remember that she lived down here until Dad died, and then moved north to be nearer the bulk of her kids. I think it was shortly after you came here. I was okay with that decision, by the way, and we've seen each other over those years. Mostly I'd go to Chicago, but she came down here a couple of times, you may remember. Anyway, she's lived there so long that she wants the funeral at her parish there. Actually, we've known that for some time now."

"Sure. Thanks for letting me know. And I do remember her visiting, at least one time, anyway."

"Well, we were wondering, actually, if you'd do the funeral. It's our way of honoring her connection to St. Helena's here. My sisters have checked with her pastor and he says it's fine with him. I know it's getting near Christmas and everything, but would you do it?"

Of course he would. It wouldn't occur to him to say no, even though he admitted to himself after he'd hung up that it was *just a tad inconvenient!* It wasn't really a long discussion that he had with himself about it. *Get over it, Wintermann. You'd just like a little more time to ease into the Christmas celebrations. It won't kill you to sacrifice a little of that comfort zone for some people-patching.*

Of course, he'd do it.

It hadn't been difficult getting ready. He got a weekend replacement, and told the daily mass-goers to pray for Catherine Restorski and her family and for him too, as he traveled. Then he called St. Hilary's in Chicago to arrange his stay and, in a most congenial conversation with the pastor, learned he'd be celebrating the funeral alone. The priest gave him directions and tips about avoiding the worst metropolitan traffic. By Friday night, having packed, he was as ready as he could think to be, except for the funeral homily. And here he was on the road after Saturday morning mass and breakfast.

It was the worst time, of course, winter weather threatening to complicate any method of travel he might choose. He had opted to drive, not trusting public transportation or someone chauffeuring him about in lieu of it, either. This way he'd have more control over his comings and goings. He would take his chances with the roads. So far, it seemed a good decision. It was cold, for which he was grateful, so intense was his dislike for the heat of summer. Even so, there was no wind or snow to distract or endanger.

He prayed the rosary and then resolved to spend time mulling over his funeral words. There are few things to see along an Illinois interstate in winter, anyway. He didn't know the public radio frequencies where he might find classical music and didn't want to search for them, so he brought along tapes, ensuring music as gentle background to his homiletic musings.

Thus occupied, he paid scant attention to the barren winter landscape. The harvest well over, everywhere leveled fields were awaiting spring plowing and planting. Largely leafless trees ringing the horizon and occasional hedgerows provided the bulk of the scenery. Even towns were sparse and well off the road, only facility signs poking up near exits to suggest human presence.

He hadn't known Catherine well. More than twenty-five years earlier she had left Southern Illinois, so, aside from occasional visits, Father John's contact with her had been next to nothing. She was one of very few people with St. Helena connections, in fact, that he didn't know well or feel close to. Since he could say little about her, he decided to reflect on how death affects individuals and families. Finally satisfied with the homily, he knew there'd be time to edit it, should the wake inspire anything further.

John Wintermann was not a studious man nor much given to theory and theology, though he appreciated those who were and the thoughts they shared with folks like him in the clerical trenches. That was already his bent in seminary when he had plowed earnestly through his studies without seeing them in any light but the most pragmatic and practical. He was, in his own estimation and that of others as well, a people person, not much given to the theoretic. From time to time he'd place into memory the occasional distilled fruit of some speculation or other, but the history and evolution of such things, their intricate and filigreed inter-weavings, were never of any real interest.

Great theological names meant little to him, as a result, and the convolutions of their thoughts even less. He felt fortunate just to recognize many of the men in question – always it had been men, at least until very recently – and perhaps identify whatever it was that made them famous. Only every so often would something resonate in terms of practical ministry, and then he'd use the thought – steal it, in his words – and even thankfully acknowledge its source.

Names like Pierre Teilhard de Chardin and Alfred North Whitehead, therefore, were meaningless to him. But for all that, the French Jesuit's thoughts on evolution and the one-time atheist philosopher's search for meaning and purpose were nonetheless underpinnings to his peculiarly personal approach to ministry.

Whitehead had come to see the problem of evil as rooted in the fact that all things perish and therefore need redemption.

Teilhard's view of evolution as factual, inevitable and God-oriented from start to finish happened to coincide with Whitehead's "tender divine care that nothing be lost."

There was, in other words, a Godly spirit of care hovering over creation – much like the "warm breast and bright wings" of Gerard Manley Hopkins' Holy Ghost – lovingly guiding all things from beginning to end. Were he to be asked, John Wintermann would have seen that force, like Hopkins, as the Holy Ghost. It was this that not only gave rise and soul to his people-patching but also invested it with an urgency that made it the driving inspiration of his pastoral ministry.

A few years earlier a priest friend had mentioned that Whitehead's faith journey had been prompted by his personal discovery of that loving, caring God. While perhaps missing any deeper ramifications, Father John had quietly given thanks for the workings of the Spirit in the philosopher's life. But he also had a small, quiet realization that his people-patching was perhaps more firmly anchored in the universal scheme of things than he'd previously realized.

Indeed, God's tender wish to lose nothing and no one was itself the very heart of Father John's efforts at patching sinful or hurting souls back to wholeness. He realized that the main way God's cosmic care seems to manifest itself is through the ordinary and easily overlooked concern of one person for another. And it was this, after all, that animated his long drive north that day and his preoccupation with his homily.

He'd traveled to Chicago once as a child, but all he remembered was the lake and a museum or two. On other trips as an adult he could identify those institutions as the Field Museum of Natural History and the Museum of Science and Industry. He little remembered what he did and saw there as a child. What did remain was the memory of a time thoroughly enjoyed.

The later trips were equally enjoyable. Three times he and several classmates had enjoyed midweek stays involving baseball and other fun. Good tickets to Cardinals-Cubs games were typically hard to come by, but one of the priests had connections in the Cards' front office, so the foursome always had wonderful seats. And true to their hapless image, the Cubs had lost to their rivals – which pleased the four Redbirds fans.

But they had also enjoyed sightseeing: Buckingham Fountain – a must each time; and Grant Park concerts on two trips; the taller buildings, though the Sears Tower was the only one he could remember, going to the top of. And there was one whole glorious day at the Art Institute on their first jaunt, where he remembered especially the Impressionist collection. The trips were in summertime, so he had enjoyed the cooler Chicago weather, which he credited to Lake Michigan and perhaps Chicago's location three hundred miles north of Algoma.

There were other museums too, and they had even discovered Frank Lloyd Wright's Oak Park home, liking it so much they went again on their third trip. They trooped to numerous large, old churches and several more modern ones as well, and on the second trip they even took a day to see the archdiocesan seminary in

Mundelein, where they chanced upon a faculty member who gave them a Cook's Tour of the nearly two thousand acres. They'd seen affluent North Shore communities and Willmette's Bahai Temple. And, of course, there were restaurants, though all he could remember about them was that one was in Greektown.

He knew it naïve to think there was little more to enjoy in the vast metropolitan area, aside from theater and concert venues. There had to be much more, but he simply wasn't aware of what. And he knew that by himself he couldn't even find most places he'd already visited. Having put himself into the hands of friends earlier, he realized that if this trip were to involve something more than people-patching, he'd have to rely on the pastor or another local expert. Not likely! The pastor would surely be too busy, and he'd come on business, anyway.

On the far side of Bloomington his long and bulky frame was crying for a break, so he stopped to stretch and to hit the restroom. Then he decided to top off his tank and get a sandwich as well. Thus fortified 'til evening, he hoped St. Hilary's pastor would allow him to treat for supper at an eatery of the local priest's choosing.

During the remaining couple of hours, Algoma occupied his thoughts. There'd been only one other death since Annie Verden's in September, and things were pretty much normal again – that is, very quiet. The summer heat wave was no longer grist for the conversation mill. Crops had fetched good prices, and Father John's farmers were happy, as was he, what with colder temperatures since Annie's burial. Autumn had stretched itself out nicely, in fact, lovely weather lasting well into November and not rain or wind enough to spoil the beautiful fall scenery by dropping the leaves early. A touch out of the ordinary, that long splash of autumn in the trees, but beautiful and welcome, certainly so far as Father John was concerned.

In mid-October he had paid his promised visit to Richard Wurtz's farm, spending all afternoon and much of the evening on the slow-spoken bachelor's farm. He reacquainted himself with the lanky man's herd and shared a quiet farm supper with him. He even contributed his own homemade dessert: bread pudding with a whisky sauce. In that same month, he'd also revisited Lafe Skinner's exotic flowers and learned more about them than he thought he would. As a result, some of them graced many a weekend altar at St. Helena's, often adding their lovely aromas to the services.

Mass attendance was at presummer levels. And, with more farm money in local coffers, business in Algoma came back nicely as well. The Methodists had kept their time-honored October Mulligan, the possibility of a Buffalo Trough a tiny memory after a brief flirtation with altering their fall fundraising. The school year was nearing midpoint. And the rumor mill was unusually quiet, word of Horace Denver's art sales not yet having surfaced. Nor, for that matter, had much else of interest hove into view. Even the novelty of the Verden Mystery that had momentarily thrilled Algoma had faded, as ephemeral as fireworks in an early July sky.

Cool temperatures finally morphed into cold ones with the return of Standard Time, the fleeing sun leaving Algoma skies murkier at each day's passing. As Thanksgiving came and went, the shorter, gloomier days wore winds hinting at snow. Natives could feel it and spoke of it to one another; Father John had sensed it as well, even as he guessed the first blanketing wouldn't be large – just enough to announce winter's arrival.

He had said as much to Fred and Frieda Becker over coffee at their drugstore shortly before he drove north, on a day much too chilly for ice cream. They had agreed about the ice cream and the snow. He even lingered over a second cup, despite the absence of any really interesting news, the drugstore's atmosphere and the three friends' camaraderie proving a comfortable respite from the increasingly nippy weather.

He'd learned that their drugstore's business had increased with the closing of Young's Pharmacy in Burger, and he congratulated them on their good fortune, without disclosing anything he knew about Wes Young's decision to move out of state.

It had been weeks since any of the three had last talked to Horace, who continued to work the town's alleyways and his own junkyard. He appeared unaffected by Annie's death. Either he was truly unaware of his actual connection with the duchess or he possessed acting abilities beyond the pale. Surely the former, bank President Bob Lanner's contention to Father John not withstanding – and far better that way, in Father John's private opinion.

With December had come Advent, and the priest's concerns turned to Christmas and Midnight Mass. He was old-fashioned enough to prefer Christmas Eve mass at midnight. And since no Algoman had ever objected, leastways not strenuously, that's what each Christmas brought to St. Helena's. Were it up to Father John, there'd also be a hint of snow, but just enough for a picture-postcard holiday.

For all that, Christmas at the parish didn't change much year to year, though Father John did vary the pre-mass carols annually. That typically thirty- to forty-minute part of the program involved the people singing along with the choir up 'til "O Holy Night," Nancy Thurman's solo. That was the moment for the procession to the Christmas crib, the Christ Child held high by a specially chosen eighth grade girl for dramatic enthronement there.

Of course, the homily was also special. He'd preached a different one each of his nearly thirty years in town, he could proudly say, and crafting those words is what really took the bulk of his time in preparation for the annual feast. Thus it always was for him: the choice of carols and quality time birthing the Christmas homily.

It was the interruption of that routine that had briefly challenged his pastoral calm, an inconvenience, he'd decided, inconsequential in the face of a ministry opportunity. So here he was on the road to Chicago and, he realized with a start, suddenly on his descent to the runway, so to speak. He had reached I-294.

The part of the beltway around the city's western edge was a much busier proposition than he'd anticipated. Traffic on that scale never troubled metropolitan St. Louis. Nor did he remember such congestion from earlier trips north. But, as he reminded himself, he wasn't the driver then and wasn't paying attention. Now he had to give lots of attention to it. Still, the sea of cars kept on rolling, and he was soon switching onto the Kennedy Expressway and then in short order onto Foster Avenue.

As he accomplished each of the maneuvers laid out on the passenger seat beside him, he tried to get a mental overview of his directions. He hadn't looked at a detailed map beforehand, trusting instead to the written directions. He didn't doubt they'd get him there, but he preferred a bird's-eye picture and was determined to get one once safely inside the rectory. Somehow the route didn't seem simple and straightforward, no doubt owing to the occasional lack of through-streets and curving expressways.

After heading east on Foster for thirty blocks or more, he made a left at Lincoln onto that diagonal avenue and headed north. There just aren't many diagonals in Southern Illinois, so this felt peculiar. He went north several blocks toward Bryn Mawr, and as he drove slowly through the intersection there, he glanced left and thought he could see the church in the distance, though he wasn't certain. He remembered that he couldn't negotiate the parking area behind the rectory without going a bit further north on Lincoln and doubling back – a one-way street alongside the rectory, if he'd remembered correctly.

Sure enough, a small street sign on his left several blocks further on announced Fairfield. It turned out to be a meandering block or so, with all of St. Hilary's buildings soon enough to his immediate right. He turned into the parking area behind the rectory a few minutes after four and hoped the pastor would be in the mood for a drink.

CHAPTER II – ST. HILARY'S

It was better than that. Not only was a drink promised, but the pastor, Father Bill Smith, had also gotten a substitute for the Saturday evening mass and had set aside the entire evening. They would indeed be dining out, since the parish, like most others throughout the country by now, had no cook or housekeeper. But there was a well-stocked bar, he was told, and Father John looked forward to that drink and some conversation.

The rectory was huge by Father John's standards. Large enough for four priests, it had two-room suites and private baths for each of them, the pastor's suite noticeably larger, but the other apartments, as the pastor called them, more than adequate. Besides the accommodations on the second floor, there were also a guest room and a spacious common room.

It was to the common room that he was directed after depositing his bags. St. Hilary's was now a one-priest parish and in decline, Father John had been willing to believe, until he saw for himself that there were no signs of urban decay. Over drinks he learned that, far from being in decline, the parish had many more than two thousand families and was growing modestly. He couldn't believe one man could handle that kind of load. Chicago's size was overwhelming to a small-town denizen like himself. Obviously the size of its parishes – and staffs, too – would also take some getting used to.

The pastor was some years younger than Father John, an easy-going and easily met man. He was as tall as Father John, but thin and gracefully lanky. He told him of demographic changes in recent decades that had given the parish a multi-ethnic population, though in that respect, he said, Hilary's wasn't very different from other city parishes. The suburbs tended toward less diversity, but even there, parishes were showing signs of multiculturalization. Father John mentioned how different all that was from his diocese. The pastor agreed, indicating he'd learned as much from downstate classmates over the years. Ethnic diversity had furnished banter for many a bull session in seminary days and was still of interest, though on a more professional and serious level now.

Father John learned that the largest influx into St. Hilary's had involved Asians – Filipinos, Vietnamese, Koreans – though there were also numbers of Hispanics. Bill said such diversity was hardly unique, but it wasn't necessarily what to expect in an assignment. Numerous areas throughout the archdiocese had relatively steady populations.

Something like the Hill in St. Louis, Father John suggested, and he spoke of that Italian neighborhood. He added that diversity wasn't at all what priest friends expected down south, however understandable it might be around the air base outside Belleville. But in smaller and more relative ways, diversity was beginning to show up elsewhere. There was an Oriental face or two in Algoma now, thanks to the family that opened a Chinese restaurant there. And with cheaper taxes and real estate, Illinois communities across from St. Louis were attracting numbers of newcomers very different from their long-time residents culturally, ethnically and religiously.

"Perhaps this sort of thing isn't difficult for you, Bill, but for us it's taken some getting used to," Father John said, stretching and shifting his weight in the comfortable chair. "But tell me what day-to-day ministry is like for you. Most of my priesthood has been in towns of less than four thousand people."

"I've had similar conversations with downstate classmates over the years, John, and I've told them, as I tell you now, that ministry in Chicago is done very differently from what you know it to be in smaller population areas. Even so, like your diocese and those of my other classmates throughout Illinois, we're definitely experiencing a clergy shortage.

"We don't have the priests to minister the way we did when I was ordained. But even then it wasn't as homey-folksy as I'm told your ministry is. We know even fewer of our people on a first-name basis than we used to because we don't see them in enough ways to get to know them. That isn't to say I know none of my parishioners. I know numbers of them ... and well, at that. It's just that more and more I know less and less of them in that personal kind of way. And I'm not pleased about that. I suppose I could put it simply: since we can't change the circumstances, we're doing the best we can."

"Oh, I don't doubt that, Bill," John said. "You and most every other priest I know! I was just wondering about the personal level of ministry here. You seem to confirm my suspicions that it's more and more impersonal, so to speak."

"Put that way, I guess so. But you know, even in the old days, I suspect that what we call personal ministry differs from what you know it to be now – and especially what you knew in the old days."

"That's what I'd like to hear more about, Bill. How personal is personal in Chicago?"

"Well, when I first got out of the sem, you could expect three or four guys in a typical parish. The pastor was an older man – often much older – and very much like a corporation president. I mean, he delegated a lot of day-to-day stuff. Usually the first assistant really ran the place, did the nitty-gritty stuff – even gave assignments to all the other priests, if the housekeeper didn't in fact run the place! The youngest or newest guy often had the youth work, for instance, and everyone had assigned mass times plus on-call time – guys out East used to call them parlor hours, I think. Anyway, each priest was available on a rotating basis a couple of hours after supper Mondays through Fridays, and sometimes Saturdays, for whatever might pop up. Given that, plus the work with special constituencies to which each of us gave most of our individual attention, we got to know a bunch of people rather well, especially since we weren't bogged down in a lot of administrative stuff – the pastor and/or the staff did that. There were also contacts at weekend masses. It was a very ordered approach that enabled lots of personal connections. Oh, you didn't know everyone by a long shot, but you knew quite a few parishioners. Between the three or four of us in a given parish, we knew almost everybody – corporately, so to speak. But today it's much more of a treadmill or an assembly line that I feel I'm working."

"Me too, in many ways," Father John interjected, sighing. "Even in our little parishes."

"And it's not just the clergy shortage, either," Bill continued. Priesting's changed since ordination: lots more meetings, committees and paperwork now; loads of stuff coming from downtown; and while any stuff like that was spread out over the several priests per parish then, with fewer guys to go around now, those time commitments are all mine. And it's a real crusher."

"Downtown?" John asked, looking puzzled.

"The chancery," Bill answered.

"Oh, okay," John said, "But as you're implying, even discounting the shortage, those changes in themselves have complicated things and cut short time for a more personalized ministry." The pastor nodded as Father John continued. "I know what you're saying. That's hit us too. And while I can still say I know all my folks, those bureaucratic things certainly enable many fewer humane contacts, in my opinion – even in our much smaller settings."

"Yeah. The combination of that and the shortage has hurt a lot," Bill said. "I think the best ministers even in the old days were something like geniuses. They had something genetic, maybe, which just made them sparkle ministerially. They knew how to reach people, encourage them, urge them, nudge them in new directions. I don't think – never did – that kind of thing can be taught. Maybe studied, but not taught. But I'm convinced today's situation is quite a bit closer to impossible, even for the geniuses – at least from what I see and experience here in the city.

"There are still successful pastors, perhaps even a good number of them. But we've redefined success. Had to. Now you've absolutely got to like meetings and committees and be good at that sort of thing – besides all the other skills you needed even just a few years back." He took a short breath. "And, it doesn't hurt to be a good preacher."

Father John's face lit up. "You've got that right. And, you know, it doesn't seem to matter how long or short you preach. Depth of thought doesn't often seem that important, either. You have to be able to reach the people in front of you in terms of their particular needs. And in terms of their abilities to pick up on what you say and how you say it. I don't know any other way to describe it, ultimately, than to call it being sincere. I know there are probably more nuances than that, but that seems to me the core of it. At least down our way."

"Well, yes. But I'd add personality. I've known bright guys who were skilled at lots of things including speaking but couldn't connect personally, no matter how hard or sincerely they tried … "

Father John cut in: "Oh, I agree. In fact, I've known fellas who could get by with anything in a parish – building projects and stuff, you know – simply because they were well-liked, while others who were less affable could absolutely not sell their parishioners on even sorely needed things that were obvious even to dolts.

"And another thing or two: we're combining parishes, which means that one priest has to learn another whole batch of peoples' names. We're also giving priests more than one parish. Same results, only worse: now there are multiple sets of meetings. It's not unusual for a man to have two parishes; some have three, and one guy has four. I don't know how they do it, and I'm quite glad I don't have to."

"We've combined some parishes up here, but few guys have more than one – at least, not yet. But it isn't getting easier. In the old days guys could afford to die with their boots on, in part because they often couldn't afford to retire and didn't know what to do if they did go that route – but especially because they had younger guys to do the heavy lifting. Now, with lots more of us as the only priest in the parish, more and more are looking to step down while they have some life left to live. And while many of the retired help on weekends, there are fewer and fewer of us actively assigned."

"Same thing down our way. But some of us are content to stick around a while longer … " John said, his voice trailing off plaintively.

There was silence for a while, Bill allowing the older man to muse a moment or two. "What kind of host am I? I haven't offered you a drink. What would you like? I'm having Scotch, I think."

"Sounds good to me. On the rocks, please," John said, his face brightening.

The Chicagoan continued: "You've not thought of retirement?"

"Oh, I've thought plenty about it. But I'm still enjoying things, and, as I said, I'm not one of those with multiple parishes or the like. You know, I worry about the guys in that boat, that, when all's said and done, they'll burn out. And then there'll just be more work for the rest of us. In a more perfect world, the powers-that-be would get to the root of what's occasioning this and try to do something about it ... "

"I know what you mean," Bill picked up the thread. "I wish somebody could figure out a solution. I don't know if marriage is the answer – not the whole answer, certainly. Anyway, do you think most guys would marry if that were suddenly allowed? I mean, of those already ordained? Not many I know up here would – some, maybe, but not most. Anyway, it still wouldn't turn things around short term."

"Yeah, I think that's so down our way too. Though the ones who would and who wouldn't marry might surprise you. What few conversations I've had with our fellas held some surprises for me. I guess I just don't know them as well as I thought I did."

Bill laughed heartily. "Hadn't given that much thought. You may be right. I wonder, now that you mention it, about several guys I know – pretty well, I think. I've got to revisit this with them."

They sipped their drinks quietly a few moments. Then Father John spoke up: "Tell me about the lady who died. She was in my parish at the start of my pastorate. Can't say I knew her well, even at that time." He snuggled comfortably down into his overstuffed chair.

"Catherine's been a delight, I must say," Bill said. "Until lately she was very involved with our ladies' group, and she was at many daily masses. Always pleasant, she was. In the last six months, though, she was around less and less as the illness progressed. She must've had cancer for several years, but you wouldn't have known it from what she did or said. Not a peep about it. First I knew of it was perhaps around Labor Day. I kept pretty close tabs after that and watched her go gently downhill. I mean to say, she was gentle in how she handled it. An inspiration, really! Do you know any of her children?"

"Just the daughter in my parish. When her mom came north to be near the other kids, Kathleen and her husband stayed. I know her mom came south a few times, but I'm pretty much in the dark about her. I only said hello those couple of times she showed up at mass on her visits. I'm sorry you can't be at the funeral, Bill, because I'm sure you'd have personal things to say that could be consoling to the family. Are you going to be at the wake? Perhaps you could do that there."

"Precisely. I'll handle that service, though I want to introduce you briefly tomorrow night. Another meeting's keeping me from the funeral, as I've already explained to her daughters. They're very understanding, and I'm grateful. That darned meeting has to do with our parish cluster: a sort of futuring moment – against the day when we have to readjust things in the area. I need to be there."

"Will the cardinal be there?" John asked, idly curious.

"Oh, no. His vicar for this area will be: an auxiliary bishop. But I hope he'll be present if and when we actually have to do something."

"You satisfied with the process for that sort of thing?"

"By and large, yeah," he said, thoughtfully. "Although I don't think you can involve the laity too much, and so far the discussions have been largely clerical."

"Same thing with us. The folks are only brought in more or less at the last moment. Not the way I'd do it if I were dictator," he said, and laughed. "Although, come to think of it, if I were dictator, I suppose I'd just raise an eyebrow, and whatever it was I thought necessary would get done – you know, boom – like that. Not good either! Let's hope I'm not promoted to dictator." He laughed again.

As the younger priest was finishing his drink, he said to Father John: "What say we get something to eat?"

"Fine with me," John said, and he gulped the last of his Scotch. "But remember, this is on me."

"We can argue about it there. There's no live entertainment, and we might put on a good show." Both men laughed, set their glasses down and went off for their coats. In the car, John said: "You know, we may go about things differently because of our different situations, but the basic stuff is the same, isn't it?" Bill agreed, smiling.

The drive was brief and the meal enjoyable: a lovely steak, quiet talk and, in the end, Dutch treat. It was the best John could negotiate.

CHAPTER III – WAKE AND FUNERAL

Father John celebrated one of the later Sunday morning masses. The pastor introduced him, and the people seemed attentive as he preached and were certainly friendly afterward at the church door. But he couldn't help feeling they'd rather have had their own priest.

The church was far larger than Algoma's. But he remembered seeing even larger ones on previous trips. He studied it carefully: research for the funeral. After mass, he and Bill went nearby for brunch, and John quizzed him about the funeral. Pretty standard stuff, he was happy to hear – nothing new to learn. Outside it was still cold: colder, it seemed, than winter temperatures in Algoma.

He spent the afternoon reading, and around 5 o'clock he and Bill went out for a light repast before the wake. The wind had picked up, and the chill seemed to go right through Father John, who wished he'd brought a heavier coat. He certainly preferred it cool, but this weather was a tad beyond his comfort zone. Tomorrow's graveside service would offer even less protection and for a longer time than just moving to and from the car. He made a mental note to ask Bill for a loaner if morning temperatures continued to be like these.

On arrival at the funeral home, he went immediately to the family and spent ten minutes with them. They seemed resigned and at peace with their mother's death, and he found the other daughters as nice as his parishioner.

When he finished, he moved to the rear of the large room and sat down to observe the crowd. He didn't know any of them, of course, and only a handful stopped to ask if he was Kathleen's pastor from down south. He noticed that the crowd was subdued and quiet, unlike the chatty folks at Feldspar's mortuary in Algoma.

Father Bill called everyone to prayer about thirty minutes later and during the brief wake service spoke movingly about Mrs. Restorski's importance to St. Hilary's. He thanked the daughters for the gift of their mother to the parish and at the end of the service introduced Father John as Kathleen's pastor from the state's southernmost diocese and the presider at the funeral mass.

Upon concluding the service, Father Bill spoke briefly with the daughters and then made his way back to Father John. "I told the girls you and I would stay only a few more minutes. They appreciated our presence, John. Do you want to tell them anything before we leave?"

"Thanks for asking, but I said everything earlier."

"Well, then, let me just work the room a little, and we'll be off," the younger priest said and moved across to first one and then another knot of people, chatting briefly with each.

In ten minutes or so, he caught John's eye, and the two edged toward the door. After a brief exchange there with the owner of the funeral home, they donned their coats and stepped outside.

"It's quite cold, Bill. Usual, this time of year?"

"Not out of the ordinary. Thank goodness there's no snow. By the way, tomorrow you'll be going up to St. Adalbert's cemetery, and immediately after, there'll be a meal at Przybylo's

White Eagle directly across Milwaukee. Hope you like CBS," he said with a twinkle in his eye.

"CBS?" Father John asked.

"Chicken, beef and sausage – typical Polish funeral fare. By the way, get ready for some stuff at graveside. Don't be surprised if things happen. The daughters probably won't prolong matters, but I suspect some of the older Poles will carry on a bit. They get emotional at graves. A good thing, I guess, to be able to vent everything."

Father John didn't know what that might entail but didn't ask. Whatever it would be, he'd been forewarned. Thus distracted, he completely forgot to mention the possibility of borrowing a coat. The two didn't stay up together that evening but went to their own rooms upon returning to Hilary's. Father John prayed compline from his breviary and went to bed early, feeling no need to rework his homily.

The next morning dawned cold again, but calm. There was no offer of breakfast, and Father John was grateful. Coffee was enough before the funeral. He spent the time checking his homily, which he'd decided still needed no changes. And once again, the matter of the coat completely escaped his memory.

The service went without a hitch, but the ride to the cemetery had been longer than he was used to, and the emotional displays at graveside were certainly new to him. They added considerably to the time they stood in the open air, but the absence of any wind made it better than he'd anticipated. As he stood waiting, he said a few private prayers of gratitude for not feeling any ill effects from the cold.

Afterward, the people gathered across Milwaukee Avenue, just as Bill had said. The food was delicious, but all John could think about was how expensive it must be to feed that many folks – in contrast to the funeral meals he was used to: parish ladies donating time and food prepared at home, with incidental expenses underwritten by the ladies' organization. It was a ministry to loyal parishioners and their families, in gratitude for many years of parish membership. Still, there was no discernible difference between the fellowship in the restaurant and that in Algoma. The people were enjoying one another and speaking words of gratitude for Stella, which was of comfort to her family.

The meal went on for nearly two hours. As it broke up, Father John declined an invitation to the home of one of Stella's daughters: "I have a return trip to prepare for. I want to get packed and go to bed early tonight. I'll leave after early mass." They understood, of course, and sent him on his way with grateful goodbyes. The funeral director had stayed for the meal and was ready to take him back to St. Hilary's.

The rest of the day was spent quietly. Bill was busy all day – first at that meeting he'd spoken of, and then with his priest support group, so John didn't expect to see him until morning. He packed, reviewed his Christmas homily, watched a little TV, grabbed a sandwich from the kitchen and went to bed early, as planned. Before sleep, he read a few chapters of the novel his friend, Father Harold Fick, had recommended. He had to admit that it was surprisingly able to hold his interest.

CHAPTER IV – DARKNESS

Father John was determined to go over to church well before the first morning mass, the one he was to celebrate so as to get an early start back home. He wanted to pray privately for a while so he was on his way downstairs more than forty minutes beforehand. The darkened rectory kitchen told him Bill hadn't yet come down to make coffee, though he'd be along soon, he presumed. He'd promised to come over to make sure the lights were on and everything was ready for mass. Pausing but a few seconds, Father John continued on toward the back door to let himself out quietly. He had in hand the key to the church that Bill had lent him on the day he arrived, and as he opened the rectory door he reminded himself of the darkness he'd encounter at that early hour.

Given the previous day's temperature, he guessed that it would still be quite cold, even more so at this early hour, and as he stepped out underneath the small overhang that protected the rear entrance, he took a deep breath to confirm his suspicions. Sure enough, the air entered his lungs spiky and sharp. He turned to his right to begin making his way to the sacristy door but stopped before taking even a step, nonplussed by the utter blackness ahead of him. There should have been light flooding the small lot where his car was parked. But it was totally, utterly dark. Instantly he remembered they were in the darkest part of the year and the dark of the moon besides. Maybe it was also overcast, for all he knew. But where was all the light that had been there the past two mornings?

He glanced to his left to see if the streetlights on Bryn Mawr were working. They were, and they cast their beams stridently in contrast to what he had just seen. But what caught his attention instead was the twinkle of tiny jewels everywhere. The patch of lawn between church and rectory was a-sparkle, as was the street beyond and the few trees he could see. It was ice, and it was everywhere. And while it was a momentarily beautiful sight, he knew in the next instant that he was fortunate not to have taken even one step out from underneath the overhang into that darkness. He could easily have slipped and fallen, and at his age, broken every bone in his body.

He still couldn't explain that darkness, especially given the proliferation of light in the distance to his left, but he determined to move up against the back wall of the church just in front of him across from the back door. He'd feel his way slowly around the corner of the building to the sacristy. He found it slick going indeed, and when he got to the corner and maneuvered around it, he realized that not even the light above the sacristy door was working, nor, for that matter, the one above the side door to the church many feet further on. He'd puzzle that out later. First, he'd open the sacristy door and get into safe territory.

But the handle was solid ice, and the lock inset into it was inaccessible. He tried several thwacks at it with his key to chip away the ice, but soon quit, fearing that he might break the key. For an instant he stood there trying to decide whether to go back into the rectory for a flashlight or to keep working with the lock. Then he thought of trying the church's side door. So he began to slowly feel his way down the side of the church wall, hoping his key would work in that lock.

When he finally reached that entrance, he stumbled over something in front of the door and nearly went down. He got his balance and then tried to brush whatever it was aside with his foot. But it wouldn't budge. Though his eyes were by then a bit more accustomed to the dark, he still couldn't make out what it was, and he paused to realign his imagination. He hadn't expected anything to be there, of course, and upon first encounter had assumed it was just a small pile of debris. Now as he rethought things and tried to re-imagine them as well, he squinted and slowly began to make out a much bigger mass on the pavement, as dark as that morning's dawn, something large, long in shape and elongated, stretched out full length. He started at the realization, finally, that it was a human body.

He reached down to find the person's head. Not wearing gloves, he found the face and touched it gently to see if he could feel breath or find a pulse. The cold feel of the skin instantly told him the person was dead. He recoiled, lifting his hand instinctively away from the face and found to his surprise that his own pulse was racing. He stood up to decide his next move and realized in an instant what it should be: he said a prayer for the person who'd probably frozen to death.

But the more he thought about it, that prospect seemed unlikely. No one would come to church the night before. And if the person had come for mass that morning, freezing to death was highly improbable in so short a time. Perhaps the person slipped on the ice and died from the fall, but even so, the lack of body heat was a puzzle. And negotiating a parking lot full of ice, not to mention icy streets and sidewalks – by car or on foot – wasn't likely either. It just didn't make much sense for a completely cold body to be lying there. But there it was, and he knew he'd better report it. He turned and gingerly made his way down the side of the church back to the rectory.

As he fumbled for his key, the rectory door opened in front of him. Pastor and visitor startled each other. The pastor grinned in recognition and said: "You're up early. Forget something?"

"You scared me. No," John said. "Actually, I'm the bearer of bad news. There's no light in the parking lot, and the locks are iced over – I can't get into church. But that's not the worst of it. There's a dead body at the side door to church."

The shocked look on Father Bill's face spoke volumes. "Dead body? Ice? Good Lord!"

"We'd better call the police," Father John said.

"Right. Come in and let's get on that. Is it a man or woman? Or a child?"

"Adult, all right. But it's so dark I couldn't tell if it's male or female. Didn't take the time to check, really. But it didn't occur to me to do that, either."

"I understand. Must have been a shock."

"Got that right. But I'm puzzled about it …"

"That's understandable. No light out there, you say?"

"Yeah, even though there's plenty of light on Bryn Mawr. On the street in front of church too, I imagine. I don't recall noticing that for sure just now, though. California, right?"

"That's right. Ice on the doors, you say?"

"On the sacristy door, for sure. Apparently we had an ice storm – the grass was all sparkly as I looked toward Bryn Mawr. And the parking lot's treacherous as can be. I inched over to church by hugging the wall the whole way." He grinned at the thought of having done that.

By now the pastor had dialed 911. Moments later he put the phone down and asked: "Coffee? Should have some in a minute or two."

Father John nodded.

"There's not much more we can do 'til the police get here. You're sure the person's dead, right?" Father John nodded. "Well, the police headlights should give us enough light. I've got a flashlight, but if it's as treacherous as you say, I'd rather wait a few minutes for the cops."

Father John agreed. "Coffee sounds great. It's downright chilly out there again. Think we should call off mass?"

"If it's that bad, I don't think anyone will make it. But we can see. Mind celebrating if anyone does show?"

"No, of course not. I'd planned to anyway, remember? And I imagine you ought to be available when the police get here. Anyway, I don't think I'll be going anywhere today," he said, smiling resignedly.

"Right. We'll make you comfortable another day or so. Whatever it takes," Bill said and paused. "But, you know, the more I think of it, I suspect they'll want to talk to you too, since you came upon the person first. We'll play mass by ear, okay? Why don't I make some signs for the church doors in case we decide to cancel everything. If it's that bad, we might just as well."

"Good idea," Father John said. "But, about that later mass – is there some way to warn folks before they get here?"

"We can put a recording on the phone 'til the staff gets here – if they do. That and the signs should do it. Not much else we can do." The pastor left the kitchen and returned shortly with paper and a magic marker. The crude signs were ready in no time. Then he recorded the message he had spoken of.

Coffee barely finished, they heard the briefest of warning pings from a siren on the small parking lot and stepped gingerly out the back door. A police cruiser was there with its lights fully illuminating the body at the side door to the church. As they joined the policemen who were by then hovering over the figure, they could easily see it was a woman in a dark-colored coat, older, even matronly, calmly lying outlined against the icy ground and glaringly out of place. She lay sprawled on the ice, her handbag still slung over her arm. The fall had caused it to slip down to her wrist and it lay near her face, which was cradled on one arm. She had a noticeable bump on her forehead but a surprisingly calm look upon her face. Father John wondered how long she'd actually been there. Then one of the policemen voiced that same question.

"Wonder when this happened. Who found her?" the older, larger one asked, looking at the two priests.

"I did," Father John said. "Fifteen or twenty minutes ago by now. No idea how long she's been there. Poor thing! Probably couldn't see a thing in this darkness."

"Yeah, I was wondering about that. What happened to the lights out here?" the younger policeman asked, looking around the lot. Neither of them seemed to mind the weather, Father John noticed. They weren't wearing gloves and seemed comfortable with their jackets partially unbuttoned.

Father Bill spoke up. "Don't know yet. I'm guessing a transformer or something like that. Rectory lights are working and the streetlights on Bryn Mawr and California. Haven't had time to check the church yet, or even report this to maintenance or the electric company. Not even sure, in fact, if my maintenance people are going to get here today. Could you call it in for us?" he asked.

"Sure, after we get a handle on this," the older cop said.

"It's a good thing school's not in session. The lights may be out in there too, for all I know," the pastor said, glancing at the school building just on the other side of the small parking area.

"Know her?" the older policeman said.

"Haven't looked closely," Father Bill said. "Excuse me. Let me step across here and take a peek at her face." He flashed a look of recognition. "It's Mrs. O'Carroll. Strange! She doesn't often come to daily mass. But that's her, all right. She just lives a couple of blocks east on Bryn Mawr. Widowed several years ago."

"I've got to check her purse," the younger cop said apologetically as he did so. In a moment he had found her wallet and verified the identification. "Suppose we'd better get her out of here. Any kin or friends we can call to break the news?"

"Don't immediately know. But I can check our records," Father Bill said. "Want to come inside for coffee while I do?"

The older policemen accepted the offer, but pulled rank and asked the younger man to stay with the body. "Shouldn't take long, right?" he asked the pastor.

"Correct."

"Want me to bring some coffee when I come back, Jim?" the older cop asked.

"Yeah. Black's fine," the young man said, gratefully. He was a nice looking, compactly built young man, probably in his late twenties.

But before the priest could lead the first officer into the rectory, Father John spoke up. "What about the church, Bill?"

"Oh, yeah. Almost overlooked that. Let us see if we can get the church open," he said to the policemen, "and check on things. You know, lights, heat … "

A quick attempt at the lock directly in front of them was successful. Somehow the ice hadn't affected that door or its lock. The policemen said they'd wait and in the meantime phone the power company, so the priests excused themselves to enter church. Exit lights above the doors were glowing and the furnace blower could be heard. Apparently light and heat weren't problems there.

"We'll unlock all the doors, and then you can wait to see if anyone comes, John." They fanned out and soon met again in the sacristy, where Bill flipped on the lights for morning mass. "If I don't get back, give it five or ten minutes beyond mass time. If no one's come by then, make your way back to the rectory. I'll put up those signs later. You can leave the doors unlocked, and don't bother with the lights, either. I'll take care of all that later."

"Right."

The pastor went to the sacristy door to open it from the inside and then used it to rejoin the policemen.

Father John checked his watch and realized the time he had set aside for pre-mass prayer was mostly eaten up. He also made a mental note to phone St. Helena's later about being delayed. Meantime, he sat in a front pew for a few minutes of praying.

His thoughts turned to the unfortunate lady outside and to her family. Some minutes later he checked his watch and looked around. The church was empty, and he could go back to the rectory. Not trusting the icy pavement outside the side door, he took the same shorter route Bill had, exiting via the sacristy. The police were still outside, and he greeted them. "Waiting for an ambulance?" he asked.

"Right. Father found a daughter a mile or so away. She's making arrangements now, in fact. Get yourself some coffee, Father. It's nice on this nippy morning," the older cop said. Both of them were nursing their own steaming mugs.

"I'm on my way," Father John shot back. "Slowly." And he chuckled.

Inside the rectory, he found the pastor in his office. "What do you want to do about the next mass, Bill? As you can guess, no one was there just now. Want me to put up those signs?"

"Would you? I'd appreciate that. I'm waiting for her daughter to call." But before Father John could get out of the room, the pastor added: "Oh, and be sure to see if the police need anything from you."

"Sure thing," John said and stepped out of the room.

In the parking lot he spoke briefly to the policemen, explaining about the signs. He'd be back soon, he told them, in case they needed any information from him. Five minutes later the three were together again beside the corpse. The sky was beginning to brighten.

"How'd you fellows get here, anyway? Everywhere it looks slicker'n a greased doorknob."

The two cops laughed. "Front-wheel drive, Father," the one named Jim said.

When he raised his eyebrows as if to begin an argument on the subject, the older policeman laughed again. "That's a joke, Father. We were on patrol when the call came, and we got right over. The streets aren't really that bad. As long as you don't do anything sudden or reckless, you can get around fine." Then, in a more business-like tone: "Tell me again exactly when you found the lady?" And he whipped out his notebook.

"As I said, perhaps ten or fifteen minutes before you arrived. I have no idea how long she'd been there. And, by the way, what's your name? I already know you're Jim," he said, indicating the younger policeman.

"Isaac, Father. So, you'd say about 5:45, then, Father?"

"That sounds right, Isaac," he said, using the man's name to help set it in his memory.

"You didn't disturb anything here at the scene, did you?"

"Well, at first I thought I'd bumped into a little debris in front of the door and tried to kick it aside. When it wouldn't budge, I bent down to check. By that time I could tell it was a body, and from the cold feel of its face, not alive. Couldn't tell if it was a man or a woman and didn't think to check. So, aside from trying to move it with my foot and touching the face, I didn't do anything else."

"Sad!" Isaac said. "All she wanted to do was go to church."

"Sure looks like it," the young one said.

Father John frowned. "What happens now? Does a funeral home pick up the body or does it go to the morgue?"

"Oh, this looks pretty clear-cut. We'll file a report, and whichever funeral home the relatives choose can get the body. We'll have to wait here 'til they arrive, which shouldn't be long now, I'm guessing."

Father John showed another small frown but held his tongue. He already had his doubts about the lady intending to come to church that morning, but he figured there'd be time enough to say or do something in that regard.

It was only later, once the police were gone and he'd had time to think about it, that he questioned the wisdom of not speaking up while the body was present. In fact, he began to stew about it a little later that morning. He'd already called Algoma to say he wasn't sure when he could get away and to promise to let them know as soon as he knew something. With Bill trying to phone his staff and make a few other calls as well, Father John had plenty of time to stew.

Maybe I need to say something in time for an autopsy before they begin to embalm her. If I'm right, she's been dead much longer than the police seem to figure. He thought that after Annie's death, his flirtation with intrigue and mystery had been satiated, but here he was back in the middle of something and taking to it rather eagerly.

Fortunately, he didn't have much longer to fuss over it. Around ten o'clock, Bill reached him on the intercom to say he'd had a call from the lady's daughter. She was ordering an autopsy.

"I'll be right down," John said.

"Know why, exactly?" Father John asked, as he entered Bill's office.

"Not sure. She probably thought something was odd about it all."

"Well, I did too – do too," Father John corrected himself. "I can't really believe she came to early mass through all those icy streets."

"Now that you mention it, that does strain credibility. Don't know why I didn't think of that myself. Probably too busy worrying about masses and my staff," he mused half to himself.

"Did any of them make it in, by the way? Your staff?"

"No. And when I got a few of them on the phone, I told them not to bother."

"Sounds reasonable. By the way, do you think I could talk to the daughter?"

"Sure. I've got her number here somewhere," he said, and began fumbling around his desktop. "Here it is. Knew I had it somewhere."

"Thanks." As he took the paper from Bill, Father John said: "I'll go over to the other office so I don't disturb you." But he was also hoping for some privacy when he talked with the lady. In a few moments he'd reached her residence but only got a recording, so he left his name and the rectory number. He told her he was hoping they could talk soon.

But that was not to happen. It was very late in the afternoon before she returned the call, which was taken by the high school student Bill had answering phones for the rest of the day. For all Father John knew, the young man was a regular, because he certainly didn't seem nervous or lacking in poise when he and Father John finally connected after supper. The two priests had meanwhile gone literally across the street to a parishioner's home for a nice evening meal. Father John was grateful for the home-cooked food but also for not having to negotiate more of the icy streets than that short walk.

When he and the daughter were finally able to talk, he told her of his suspicions. "I can't really believe your mother would have dared all those slippery streets to come to mass. And that early, besides."

The daughter was in agreement. "It wasn't like Mom to go to the early mass anyway, and especially on such a bad day. The two policemen told me that they thought something wasn't right either.

38

In fact, they encouraged me to have an autopsy, and while they said they wouldn't write up the incident as criminal or even suspicious, they thought something was fishy."

"Interesting! I didn't mention anything to them, nor did they say anything like that to me. But then, I wouldn't have been quite the appropriate person. You were, and I'm glad they spoke up to you. When I noticed there was no warmth whatever to her face, I was pretty sure she'd been gone a long while by the time I got to her. And it didn't make sense finding her like that outside church. But, just to cover all the bases, might she have come to church last night for any reason?"

"I don't think so, Father. There was nothing particular going on that I'm aware of. Perhaps you can verify that with Father Bill."

"Good idea. Give me a moment." A quick chat with the pastor confirmed that, and Father John went back on the phone.

"Do you think, then, Father, that there was foul play?"

"Well, I'd hate to rush to that judgment. Why not wait for the postmortem? When do you think you'll know?" Father John was keeping his direst thoughts to himself, in part because it was probably too hasty, but also to spare the daughter needless worry.

As he was conversing, Father John kept trying to get a mental picture of the lady. She was poised, especially under the circumstances, and he envisioned an attractive, middle-aged woman of above average height who presented a pretty and pleasant figure.

"By the time I got connected with the proper people, Father," she said, "it was early afternoon. But I told the morticians right away to hold off embalming, and I'm glad I did. Besides, we have out-of-town relatives who can't get here very quickly, so another day won't hurt a thing. The medical people said they might not be able to do the procedure 'til tomorrow, and it looks like that's what's going to be happening. I'm also not sure how long that takes or how quickly they can generate a report."

"It shouldn't take that long," the priest said. "Even if they don't get to it today, you should still know well before tomorrow evening, unless I'm mistaken. If they call you right away, that is."

"Oh, they promised to call me. Well, we're still making arrangements, and, as I said, a little extra time won't hurt. There are those out-of-town relatives, and the roads are an issue too. We also have to juggle it all with Christmas in mind, you know. So it's a crapshoot. Anyway, one more day won't matter."

"I hope doing all that won't prove too much for you. You've got to be upset at a time like this. But, if you can stand my curiosity, would you mind sharing those results with me?"

"Not at all, Father. Thanks for your concern. Good night."

As he hung up, Father John couldn't escape the feeling that something was rotten in Denmark. But he wouldn't know for sure until tomorrow, if then. Anyway, he wouldn't be leaving for Algoma just yet.

CHAPTER V – IN CONFERENCE

The next morning the two priests concelebrated the later morning mass, Bill having cancelled the early one. Even so, there weren't many people present. Father John marveled that anyone made it at all. Afterward, they both agreed that coffee, toast and juice in the rectory would be enough, and after that meager meal, the pastor headed to his office to begin recovering the rhythm of parish work. One or two staffers had made it in that morning, and things were struggling back to normalcy at St. Hilary's.

Some minutes after eleven, the pastor's voice sounded from the intercom in Father John's room. "There's a call for you, John."

"For me? You sure?"

"Right."

Must be Algoma – or maybe the daughter. "Can I take it here?" he asked.

"Right. Just push the button by the blinking light."

He picked up the receiver only to hear an unfamiliar male voice ask tentatively: "Are you the priest who celebrated the funeral yesterday?"

"Yes. I'm Father John Wintermann. How can I help you?" he said, relieved it wasn't bad news from down south. *This is intriguing. Wonder if he wants a copy of my sermon.*

"I attended the funeral, Father, and I was impressed. Can we talk sometime today? I realize you're from out of town, but I'm glad you're still around. I imagine the weather's kept you here."

"Right. I'm guessing you probably can't get around in this ice, so go ahead."

"Oh, no. I can. What I mean is, I'm not that far from you and can walk over. It'll take a little while, but if it's all right with you, that's what I'd like to do."

"Fine with me, but two questions first. When do you think you'll make it, and what do you wish to discuss?"

"I figure I can be there a little after noon, say, twelve-thirty, one o'clock. I'd like to go to confession."

"Well, certainly. I'll be here. Just ring the front doorbell. I'll alert the pastor that I'm expecting someone." *No sense his bumping into Bill if he's trying to confess to a stranger.*

"Good. See you, then, Father … John … right?"

"Right. 'Til around one, then." As he hung up, he couldn't help thinking that the young man – the voice sounded young – must certainly feel a strong need for forgiveness if he's willing to brave all the ice like that.

Not sure how to use the intercom, he went downstairs to tell Bill about the appointment and had to wait for him to finish yet another phone call. After he'd told him, Bill asked about lunch.

"I thought you didn't have a cook. Do you have food in the house we can fix?"

"Not really. But if I lean on someone – and if I call now to give him enough time – we might get something delivered by noon."

"In this weather?" John asked in disbelief.

"Well, yes. I think it can be done. If you're game, we can at least check it out. Sandwiches okay?"

"Sure. Want me to stick around while you try?"

"Yeah, stay a moment – for menu choices."

Father John smiled. He sat down beside the desk and began thinking about what he might like to have. *Something healthy – turkey, maybe.* He waited while the pastor found a number and dialed.

Within minutes he'd been assured that with this much notice something could be readied and probably be gotten to them by noon. No promises as to an exact time, but soon seemed possible.

"Good. Call if you can't swing it," he said and hung up. "All things come to good ..." he said. John's knowing smile assured Bill he needn't finish the quote from St. Paul.

The food arrived a few minutes after the noon hour, and the young man who brought it said that it was still a little tricky outside, so he was glad there weren't many people driving around. The turkey tasted particularly good, and it filled the void his breakfast hadn't even dented.

When the doorbell sounded about quarter to one, John said: "Early! I'll get it. If it is for me, may I use the front parlor – office – whatever you call it?"

"Sure. But if it's for me, just shout," Bill said, and began clearing the table. He had sent his two staffers home early because things were slow, so the two priests were the only ones in the rectory.

At the door, a man tentatively introduced himself as Michael and asked if he could come in.

"Of course. You called earlier, right? I'm Father John Wintermann."

"Yes, I did, Father. Thanks for seeing me."

"This way. There's a room right here. Watch your step," he said, shaking the man's hand and then ushering him up the several steps into the lobby.

They settled into chairs in the small office, Father John moving his out from behind the desk to be alongside the other man, who, while young, wasn't as young as he'd sounded on the phone. *Perhaps in his mid-forties – not that it really matters.* He was sturdily built, with a high forehead and what seemed to Father John to be compassionate eyes.

"Tell me what's on your mind."

"Well, it's a long story, Father – and complicated. I'd like to tell it my own way, if that's all right."

"You've got the floor," the priest said, grinning. "And my ear."

"Thanks. My name is Michael, as I said. Michael Partland." He looked very earnest. Father John liked him immediately. "Thanks again for seeing me. This may sound strange, but I think this all is best put into perspective. So …" He paused for a deep breath. "My father served in Korea before I was born. While I could never get much out of him about it before he died a few years ago, I was able to piece together the things I did get over the years – from him and others, including my mom. I began to figure there was more of a story than he'd been telling most people, even our family. There were just the three of us, by the way. And I'm adopted, which is important, as you'll see.

"Anyway, he died a lingering death from cancer, so I had a bunch of occasions to talk with him in his last months. I kept trying to pry things out of him, but never got much. Not enough, anyway, to my liking. One thing I was able to get was that he served in combat as a corporal under a Sergeant O'Carroll."

Nothing flickered on the priest's face, but his mind was now beginning to race. He'd noticed that Michael's initial nervousness appeared to be settling down, and the twitch in his right hand had disappeared. But he'd just said a magic word, "O'Carroll," and the priest tried to listen even more closely now.

Michael continued. "After Dad died, some time went by settling the estate and helping Mom move on emotionally. But I finally got time to start checking out people in the city with that last name. I must have showed up at sixty doors or more over the last couple of years. I didn't want to do it by phone – I wanted to read their facial reactions, you know? I'd found out that Sergeant O'Carroll was from the city – at least originally. Couldn't be sure, of course, if he was still around or even still alive, but I kept checking. No luck, though, those two years. I used the phone book as my guide, crossing off names as I got to them.

"You have any idea how many O'Carrolls are in Chicago, city and burbs, Father? Way too many to find a needle in a haystack, and my haystack was enormous. I was going to have to get lucky.

"Well, Monday, I finally did. Mom knew the woman you buried – they'd worked together in political campaigns a long time back – so we went to her funeral. You came across as very kind, Father. It's why I searched you out today. Afterward, I took Mom to see friends nearby and told her I was going to look around on my O'Carroll search. She laughed. She keeps telling me I'm obsessed over something not all that important, let alone possible. Anyway, I tried two places within several miles of here and struck out again. But then I came back this way for Mom and stopped at one more house – on Bryn Mawr: Irene O'Carroll's." He was watching the priest's face closely now – still nothing there.

"Like most people I've met doing this, she was hesitant when I started my little canned story. In fact, she looked even more nervous and uncertain than most of the people I've met these past couple of years. But when I got to the Korean War part, she brightened up.

"She said that her husband had served with a Walter Partland.

"I told her that was my father's name and explained that I was in the area for the funeral but had to take Mom back home, and I asked if I could return in a couple of hours, and she said that would be fine.

"So that's what I did. But on the way, on the way home, Mom now seemed to be thinking my quest wasn't all that silly. She showed no little interest in what the lady might have to say about Dad and his war service. And only then did I begin to suspect that Dad had maybe told her things that he – and she – hadn't told me. Turned out I was right, but Mom didn't know everything I was about to learn.

"I dropped her off and came back up here – we live on the South Side, Father, in St. Sabina's Parish. By the time I got back here it was getting late, well after four o'clock, and starting to get dark.

"The lady was very gracious. When we sat down she offered coffee. And I told her what little I knew about Korea, including that Dad had served with a man named O'Carroll, his sergeant."

"'That's right,' she said. 'My husband was a sergeant in Korea – left the Army as a master sergeant, in fact.'

"Well," I said, "I wonder what else you know about Dad. Maybe your husband told you a few things I don't know."

Father John had begun to listen as though he were in the room with the two of them. He pictured the lady speaking softly to Michael, who, in turn, was earnest and anxious. He forgot about watching Michael closely, so totally was he caught up in the narrative.

"'As a matter of fact, he did speak of your father,' she said. 'As he told it to me, they were very close – good friends.'

"Before she could go on, I interrupted: 'But they never contacted each other after the war – not that I know of, anyway – and I learned about your husband only a few months before Dad died. And it came from an aside, really. He just mentioned it sort of in passing.'

"'I'm afraid it may sound strange, but I think I know the reason for that – or maybe several reasons. It has to do, in part at least, with a very intense battle they were in together.' My anxious look prompted her to quickly add: 'Oh, they didn't lose their friendship over it or anything like that. But it was a very sad and strange day.

"'They were engaged with the Chinese. And while theirs was a commanding position, they couldn't maneuver much because of heavy enemy fire – and they were determined to hold the hill they occupied. As my Pat described it, they were well fortified and dug in, and reinforcements were promised. But with the Chinese, you never knew. They had enormous numbers and didn't seem to mind losing a lot of troops to achieve something. So our side could hardly be sure of the outcome, and that made troops up and down the line jumpy beyond ordinary battle nerves. More and more that was how the Americans felt whenever they encountered the Chinese, very edgy.

"'Anyway, the battle had gone on intermittently for two days and nights, and several times the Reds had launched probes in the dark, hoping to surprise us. Each time they were repulsed. Then they tried again, coming well before dawn the third morning. This time they succeeded in getting much closer to our lines than before and to the machine-gun position your father and my husband were manning – or, I should say more precisely, my husband was manning and your father was assisting at, because Walter was feeding ammunition into Pat's gun.

"'They'd been shooting so much the gun was near to overheating, and Pat was worried what might happen if they had to stop firing to let it cool off. I suppose your dad was worried too, but Pat didn't mention that. It was winter, very cold, and there was snow on the ground, and neither of them knew what might happen if they used a little snow to cool off the gun. The barrel might explode or something. Anyway, your dad began to do that, a little at a time, and it seemed to help. So they were able to keep shooting at the Chinese. They couldn't imagine where they were all coming from, there were so many.

"'They'd been at it long enough for morning to break over the eastern hills, and then they could see clearer what appeared to be no end to the depth of the Communist force. They just kept hammering away at us and didn't even seem that interested in keeping under much cover, either. That also didn't help American morale, even though we'd killed hundreds of them – bodies were everywhere. Pat said it was like eighteenth-century warfare: just line 'em up and mow 'em down. And now they could see more or less everything that was happening: where the enemy was, what strength they were coming at them with, how close they were getting. It was totally scary, according to my husband.

"'Then several different positions to the left of them took significant hits, and one, maybe two, machine-guns were knocked out. The gunners were all killed, their support troops too. There was this rather sudden break in our line, and when the Chinese realized that shooting from that sector had ceased, they redoubled their efforts up the hill in that direction.

"'Crossing fire from guns on either side of the hole, including the gun position your dad and Pat were occupying, began to sweep the advancing line, but those gunners had to worry about their primary targets directly in front of them too. Frantic requests for help were made to the rear.

"'Well, with the coming of light, we were beginning to get air support, which helped significantly. But the Communist advance kept inching closer, concentrating now on that breach in our line. From the rear we got mortar fire brought into the area around the hole, even falling very close to our troops along the battle line. It all helped, but just to slow the advance, not to stop it. It got so bad, Pat told me, that the Chinese were using their dead as temporary shields on their way up the hill, stopping momentarily to get off some shots and then creeping forward again, moving from body to body.'

"Irene noticed my rapt attention and stopped to ask: 'Didn't your father tell you about this firefight?'

"'Not one word.'

"She looked mildly surprised, but continued.

"'Well, it got worse. By 9:30 the Chinese were maybe seventy yards away. And they started that yelling thing they did before a direct charge. It was meant to frighten, of course. And Pat said it did. But when there was no charge after perhaps a minute of noise, word went up and down our line to calm down. And the men gradually did. Then, during a lull in the bombardment by our planes, in came several MiGs. They didn't attack the area where Pat and your dad were, but they hit positions further to the left of the hole in the American line, still gaping there and virtually undefended – we hadn't yet re-enforced it. So the fear returned, because our guys figured the Reds were coming as soon as the MiGs left. But that didn't happen immediately, either. And Pat said that to this day he – and everybody else, too – could not figure out why they let that time go by. Bad coordination, maybe, but certainly highly unusual – and very poor militarily.

"'In another couple of minutes, the enemy charge finally began – or, at least, a portion of the enemy line came up the hill at the opening. The whole enemy line didn't come, but the center of it began to advance. And just as it did, our troops finally got there from the rear. Pat said it was like a Western movie when the cavalry comes in the nick of time. They didn't even have time to dig in, but they surprised the Communists anyway – the Reds weren't expecting to meet anyone in that sector, of course. And in the next few minutes, all hell broke loose at either edge of the hole. Their troops were fanned out not only across the breach but they overlapped onto the places where our positions had held. It looked like a wedge, Pat said. So Pat and Walter's machine-gun position was suddenly facing the onslaught from one edge of the Chinese force.'"

Michael stopped to take a breath, and looked at the priest. "I told you this was long and complicated."

"I'm not sure where this is leading, but it's powerful. Don't stop now." The priest found that his hands were tightly gripping the sides of his chair and he self-consciously relaxed them.

"Okay." Michael seemed in a zone with his story, calm and focused. After another breath, he picked up the narrative.

"By now it had gotten dark. I remember glancing at the window and feeling surprised. I was so caught up in this epic I'd never heard before that I lost track of time. Mrs. O'Carroll noticed – saw me glance at the window – so she stopped to ask if I was all right. Did I want anything? And before I could answer, she went to get more coffee for us both. Then she sat down again and started in again.

"'Let's see,' she said. 'Oh, yes. They were almost overrun – almost. Had it not been for a lot of heroics, they still would've been, despite the fresh troops. Meantime, Pat and your dad took the occasion to stop firing momentarily and lob every grenade they had – the Chinese were within range for that by then. They must've thrown six or eight down the slope within a minute's time, he told me.

"'Then they began to fire their machine-gun again. They didn't care any more if it overheated. They figured they were dead if they stopped firing anyway and might as well go down one way as another. It had gotten that bad. Later, that's what they both agreed was going through their minds: they were all out of other choices.

"'They survived, obviously, but there's much more to the story. The Chinese kept trying to advance for ten or twenty minutes, and though the troops that had just arrived helped make a difference, it was the return of our jets that finally stopped them – and none too soon, Pat felt. But not soon enough to avoid his getting a shoulder wound. Neither he nor Walter could know at the time, but the wound wasn't that serious. The huge amount of blood suggested otherwise, so they were under even more stress the final minutes of that firefight.

"'You see, your dad not only helped stop Pat's bleeding, but he did it in between getting off short bursts from the machine-gun – enough to convince the Chinese that it was business as usual at their position. Machine-gunners, perhaps you know already, don't just shoot indiscriminately. They're often quite deliberate about their targets, and they vary their patterns as well. Sometimes it's short bursts, sometimes they sweep an area, and sometimes they concentrate their fire in a relatively small area. So the Reds couldn't tell from his sporadic fire pattern what he was up to. They thought the gunner's entire attention was on them. They didn't realize how distracted your dad was at the time.

"'When the Chinese finally retreated back down the hill, they'd been at it over six hours – since about four in the morning. When it became clear there was an actual lull, the Americans regrouped. The wounded were evacuated and other troops were able to relieve our men all up and down the line. Pat was evacuated to the rear with the wounded. And your dad stayed right beside him.

"'Some colonels were going around among the weary and wounded to determine who'd get medals. They awarded Silver Stars on the spot to Pat and to the gunner on the other side of the hole. Pat also got a Purple Heart, of course. He said he thought at the time that your dad was included in those awards. He understood that medals were due everyone in both gun emplacements – the living and even the dead. Only later – much later – did he find out otherwise, and he felt bad about it, especially about your father. But he always judged later that there was little he could have done at the time – for numerous reasons.

"'First off, your dad went back into the line within a day or two, and Pat was moved even sooner than that to a hospital far to the rear. So they were soon separated and couldn't talk further. In fact, they weren't together again in Korea. And a lot of time also went by before Pat actually learned your dad had been excluded. Then too, Pat found out that there was some Army politics concerning those battle citations, and the colonel wasn't about to change his mind once he'd signed off on them. But finally, and especially, Pat discovered that Walter had gotten on the wrong side of that colonel. That may have been the determining factor, in fact.

"'None of that sounded promising for your dad getting a battle citation. In Pat's mind, however, he deserved one. He'd been as brave under fire as any of the men that day and, as Pat saw it, he'd also saved his life. But a medal wasn't to happen.'

"'But that could have been addressed later, couldn't it? I mean, Dad deserved that commendation, right?'

"'Yes, and yes. But Pat didn't do any such thing.'

"'Why? Do you know?'

"'I think so.'

"'He didn't tell you?'

"'Not in so many words. But I think I know why. I can tell you, he thought about it afterward, while he was still in service, even. He did speak of that to me. And he continued to think about it after the war. I know, because we spoke a little about that on occasion too. He even went so far as to write a lengthy letter to the Defense Department. But he never sent it. Eventually he thought too much time had gone by for the Army to care any longer. 'They won't bother now,' he told me several times. So the best I've been able to do is to try figuring out his mind.'

"'And … ?'

"'I think part of it was that by then – well after the war – Pat was embarrassed. And he didn't know how to get past that. I've always believed – I told him this more than once – that he should have at least up and talked to your dad. His flip answer was he didn't know where he was by then. While that was true, he could have found him – if in no other way, through the VA. But he wouldn't try.'

"She paused. 'But, you know, he never destroyed that letter.'

"'The one intended for Washington?'

"'Yes.'

"'You still have it?' I asked, hopefully.

"'I do. Would you like to see it?'

"'Oh, yes,' I said, with unrestrained emotion.

"'It's here in our Bible. I'll get it.' She rose and retrieved the large family Bible from the coffee table. 'I keep it in here ... with other important things,' she said, and handed him a crisply folded piece of paper. She waited while he read it. 'I have no real use for it any more. Would you like to ... to have it?'

"I didn't reply immediately. I was still reading the letter as she returned the Bible to the table. Then I reread it before looking up. I was gazing into the distance and said, slowly and distractedly, 'Yes. Of course, I'd like it.' I kept gazing, lost in thought a few more moments. Then I turned to Irene and said with deep feeling: 'My father *is* a hero.'"

CHAPTER VI – AGONY PROLONGED

Michael gave a surprised look at his watch and then glanced at the priest. Before he could say anything, Father John said: "You all right? That's pretty dramatic stuff. Why'd you stop?"

"Sorry. Think I've done it again: lost track of time. I imagine you might want a break."

"Not really. You?"

"Well, I could use something to drink, Father. But … not here. I don't want to put you to the trouble. Besides, there's a lot more to this story. Why not let's go somewhere for coffee or something?"

"In this weather? It's icier'n a stepmother's stare out there."

"Not as bad as you think. Take your time and it's all right. After all, I got here, didn't I? And all the way from the South Side, too."

"Good point. I guess we could do that. Are you sure it's safe? Besides, is anything even open?"

"I imagine so – there was traffic around about. Let's try it. Okay?"

"Well, I suppose … "

"Good," Michael said before the priest could change his mind. "I'll get my car – it's parked back up the street on Fairfield. I'll come to the corner and honk. But watch your step. Slow and easy does it when you're walking."

"Oh, I'll just go out with you now and wait on the corner, if that's all right."

"Sure. It'll only take a minute to get the car." The young man was already putting his coat on.

"I'll just have to go upstairs to get mine," Father John said.

"Then come out when you can. I'll go fetch the car." He seemed in a very determined hurry.

Moments later when Father John stepped outside, he was surprised at how bright it was. He hadn't so much as glimpsed the outdoors since morning mass. It was still cold, but it nonetheless felt like the ice could be melting. *Or maybe that's just wishful thinking.* He could see that Bryn Mawr had been salted and was drivable, though Fairfield, the street alongside the rectory, didn't look that good. He was soon sitting in Michael's blue Olds.

"Where to?"

"Over to Lincoln. There are places all along there."

"Be careful," the priest cautioned.

Michael laughed. "I will. I've been out already – remember? The major streets are pretty much okay. Much better than yesterday. We shouldn't have any problem. Restaurants shouldn't be crowded, either."

He was right. He drove slowly and they were soon parked outside a small cafe a few blocks away. It had been simple. Father John wondered if the highways were as negotiable and whether he might have been able to go home after all. But he dismissed the thought. He was obviously meant to stay: to be of help to Michael. He was crediting the Holy Spirit with keeping him in Chicago.

Michael was also right about the crowds. There were only several other midafternoon patrons, and the two men got a table in the back with almost total privacy.

While they awaited their coffee, Father John used the facilities. A steaming cup was there when he returned, and he sipped it gratefully. Michael seemed in no hurry to continue his tale, so Father John seized the moment for a few personal questions.

"You said you were adopted. Tell me about that."

"Well, it's jumping the gun, maybe, but what do you want to know?"

"Well, you're an only child, then?"

"Yes."

"Adopted at birth, I suppose."

"Interesting question! No. I was a couple of years old. And my folks got me when Dad returned from the service. But, you know, they're the only parents I remember."

"When he returned? Not after?"

"Yeah. Pretty much right away. I guess they knew they couldn't have children. They applied almost immediately, and I arrived in short order, I was told. It's more complicated today, I believe. Takes longer."

"Right. It's far more complicated. But pardon my curiosity about something else. When did they tell you about the adoption?"

"From early on they talked of it. They told me I was special. And I liked that. Still do."

"What a nice way to handle it. But, tell me, why is it jumping the gun to ask about it now? Is it part of your long and complicated story?" He hoped he hadn't sounded like he was mocking the young man.

"You'll see."

"You're teasing! Okay. Let's switch gears, then. You spoke of confession … "

"I'm getting to that too. I said this was long and complicated."

Perhaps he's mocking me. "You did. But I'm wondering if we'll have to rent you a room at the rectory before this gets finished," the priest said, and grinned.

"I'm gettin' there! Let me continue the story."

"Fine." Father John grinned again.

"Where was I?"

"The letter about your father."

"Oh, yeah. Mrs. O'Carroll asked if I wanted it, and I said yes, of course. I have it with me here, in fact. Wanna read it?"

"No need. Just tell me the main points."

"Her husband goes into detail about the battle, how heroic Dad was, saving his life and all. And he ends with a plea – not a request, a plea – that the medal thing be reconsidered." His voice broke, and he blinked back tears. "Sorry. It got to me yesterday, and now it's getting me again," he said, and withdrew into silence.

Father John sat patiently allowing him his grief – or pride – and studied the younger man. He had a very pleasant face, even though right now it was creased with emotion. He had a modest demeanor to him, as though he was deferential in his usual dealings with other people.

When Michael looked up again, Father John quietly asked, "What happened next?"

"Mrs. O'Carroll said I was welcome to it. I got up and put it in my jacket by her front door. When I came back and sat down, she asked somewhat hesitantly if I'd like to eat a little something. It had gotten past suppertime, and it didn't take long to decide. I phoned Mom so she wouldn't worry, and when I was sure it was all right with her, I agreed to stay. Actually, Irene seemed like she might also have more to say, though I couldn't imagine what. Far as I could tell, she'd said all there was to say about Dad by then.

"We had a nice bowl of homemade vegetable soup. There was nothing memorable about the food or the conversation, but it was pleasant and folksy. I learned how she and Pat met. She told me of the daughter they had right after the war, and then of their son several years after that – and how he died from a college football injury. She said Pat's last years were spent in declining health – he died a couple of years ago, but it was nothing to do with his war wound. His lungs, I believe. For all that, I must say Irene still looked quite healthy last night, especially given her age."

The priest couldn't help noting the words about her health, but said nothing. He had been wondering the whole time if he was going to hear the sin of murder confessed. Somehow, the young man didn't seem the type, and the story he was telling didn't support that either. He refocused his attention on Michael as he continued with his tale.

"I'd noticed earlier how exceptionally neat her place was – scrubby-Dutch, as my Mom might say. And I smiled to myself when she told me her maiden name: Nenninger – German, I guess you realize. I volunteered to help with the dishes, and as we were putting away the few we'd used, Irene grew noticeably quieter by the minute. I thought she simply couldn't think of anything more to keep the conversation going, so I made up my mind to thank her as soon as the opportunity presented itself and tell her I'd be going home. But as we walked into the front room, she asked me to sit down. What she then revealed to me was startling.

"'I was frightened when you said your name at the door,' Irene said.

"'I guess so, your having that letter, and all.'

"'No, not that. I was afraid you'd come for a different purpose.'"

Michael suddenly stopped. Father John had been staring out the front window of the restaurant and listening intently. And when Michael's voice ceased, he shifted his focus to look directly at the younger man, whose face had contorted into … Father John wasn't sure what. Then, abruptly, Michael began to cry.

Father John was caught off-guard and didn't know what to do. He thought momentarily that he had triggered it – but soon dismissed that. So he sat silently, waiting for an explanation from Michael.

When it didn't come and the tears didn't cease, he reached across and took his companion's hand, but Michael pulled his back – and continued crying. So again Father John sat and waited.

When at last Michael was able to speak, he said faintly, "I'm sorry, but I don't think I can continue right now."

"That's okay, I can wait, Michael," the priest said.

"No, I mean I can't continue tonight."

"Michael, is it something I said or did? I'm sorry if … "

"No," Michael said hastily. It's … it's just getting to me. I have to pull back."

"Certainly, whatever you want or need. Do you wish to make that confession before we quit here today?"

"No," Michael said, a little hastily, it seemed to Father John.

"Okay, then. Do you think you'll be able to continue tomorrow?"

"I hope so. Let me go to the washroom a moment," he said, even as he was rising to head in that direction. Father John was left sitting there bewildered and tempted to blame himself for something, he wasn't sure what.

When Michael returned, his face had been splashed with water and he looked relatively composed. All he said was, "Let me get you back to St. Hilary's." He threw several bills onto the table and made rather abruptly for the door. Father John scrambled to grab his coat and follow.

By the time he reached Michael's car, the engine had already come to life, and he barely got his door closed behind him when Michael pulled cautiously away from the curb. Whatever the hurry was all about, Michael certainly seemed in a rush. Father John thought better about questioning it or even commenting on it, and sat in silence as they made their way back up Lincoln to turn onto Fairfield.

At the front door to the rectory, Father John asked before getting out: "Will you call tomorrow, or do you perhaps want to set up a time now?"

"I'll call, Father. I'm sorry, but this is just getting to me. I hope I'll feel better tomorrow." And during the brief but awkward silence that followed, Father John finally opened his door and got out.

"Goodbye, Michael," he said. "Please do contact me tomorrow – anytime after 9 o'clock, because Father Bill and I will probably have the later mass together. I'll be waiting for your call."

He'd barely gotten the words out when Michael's car started to inch forward. He had just enough time to close the door of the Olds before it was moving at some speed toward Bryn Mawr. Father John stood there alongside the curb, worried about the unshriven young man and fearing the worst for him. He had asked for confession, after all, and with Mrs. O'Carroll dead, it might be for the sin of murder, for all the priest knew. The issue was hardly rash judgment but rather a concern for a soul in need of the sacrament of forgiveness. Father John could care less what the sin was, but if it was serious, he wanted very much to offer the church's forgiveness. And he had been unable to do that.

What's his hurry? It must have been me. But ... what did I do? It was disturbing to Father John, who had nothing to do now but turn and go inside.

He was grateful there were no messages, but neither was Father Bill around. So he went upstairs to his room to pray and to brood, more or less in that order, though the brooding was punctuated by several more prayerful moments.

No sense emerged from the muddle he felt mired in. He eventually wandered into the kitchen to scavenge something, after which he went back upstairs. He watched the evening news and finally heard Bill come in the back door. But he was still so flummoxed by the events of the afternoon, that all he did was get the next morning's agenda from him: they would be concelebrating the later mass, just as he'd thought. And then he announced that he was retiring early.

He tried to doze off but had little success. Sleep eluded him for several more hours.

CHAPTER VII – WAITING

The morning of the twenty-first dawned cold but clear. Gone was the overcast of the previous day. Ice was still evident everywhere, but it had lost its luster, perhaps because of urban grime. Or maybe it was really starting to thaw. The absence of wind was also obvious to Father John as he made his way to the sacristy for mass. *If it would warm up some, I'm sure I'd be able to drive safely.* It was, after all, getting closer to Christmas Eve. Even so, he felt he couldn't go without seeing things to a close for Michael and for Irene and her daughter.

Michael was not at mass, not that Father John really expected that. But he could hope, he told himself, and he'd been discreetly looking for him. *Let's hope he calls at least – and soon.*

But the call that came over his après-mass coffee was not from Michael. It was Irene's daughter.

"Hello, Father."

"Oh. Do you have results already?" Father John asked, recovering from his surprise at hearing a woman's voice.

"No. Sorry to have gotten your hopes up. This is something else. I was wondering … " she said, her voice trailing off.

Father John said: "What?"

"Well," she said, and paused again, then blurted out: "Do you know anything about the man who is Mom's next-door neighbor?" When Father John was momentarily speechless, she added: "Maybe I shouldn't bother you with this now … "

"No, it's fine. It's just that I don't know anything about him, is all. Why?"

"Well, he's kind of weird."

"Did you order the autopsy because you thought it odd of your mom to come to the early mass? Or did you have another reason? Or other reasons, maybe? Like that neighbor?"

"Well, this neighbor's been in the back of my mind, yes."

"You think he did something, maybe?"

"Yes, maybe. The autopsy couldn't hurt, I figured."

"Right, it can't. It *is* an extra expense, but it will lay any doubts to rest. So tell me about that neighbor, if you'd like."

"He got upset with Mom a few years back – about a tree in her yard dropping fruit and leaves and an occasional limb onto his side of the fence. He got pretty nasty. And while Mom always tried to be nice to him, especially after that argument, he hasn't been very nice to her – nothing physical, but lots of verbal abuse. And lately – maybe the past year – he has barely spoken, has gone out of his way, in fact, not to. He's a big man, and ten years or more younger than Mom. Kind of frightening, when you think about it."

"You hadn't thought about him before?"

"Well, not lately, for sure. And not seriously 'til Mom's death Tuesday."

"Think he's the kind of guy who might do something to her?"

"Well, the thought crossed my mind, yes."

"Have you told the police? Now or ever before?"

"I haven't. I don't know about Mom. But knowing her, she probably didn't either."

"Why not let's wait for that autopsy? It may rule out that sort of thing, you know. Another day can't hurt, right?"

"I suppose so. I can wait. It's just that he's so big and potentially dangerous, you know, and I was really wondering what you might think. I hadn't taken him very seriously 'til now. And he's certainly strange. I mean, he lives alone, is a relatively recent immigrant – Eastern Europe, I think. He's hard to understand, given his accent, and I don't know how well he fits into our society, which may make him a little quick to protect himself and his interests, it seems to me. He's certainly aggressive. It shows in what he does and says, and how he says it. He's abrupt and loud. All that, you know what I mean?"

"I can see where such a person would leap to mind at a time like this. Have you any way of knowing if he's aware of your mom's death? That is, if he's innocent – which we shouldn't rule out."

"I can't be sure, but maybe not. Nothing's really happened at Mom's place to indicate anything, I believe. And it's not in the paper yet."

"Well, let's wait for that report, then. Okay?"

"Okay. But do you think I should maybe tell the police about him?"

"As I said, we need to see those results first."

"That's what I'll do, then. Thanks for listening. I'll call as soon as I hear something."

"With everything on your mind, that's very kind. I'll await word from you. Thanks again." And he hung up. But he decided to talk to Bill about this newest wrinkle. He found him in his office.

"Got a minute?"

"Yeah," the priest said, looking up from his desk. "Sit down. What's up?"

"I just talked to Irene's daughter, and she mentioned a strange man who lives next to her mother. Know anything about him?"

"A little. He's Catholic, an immigrant of a few years now, though he hasn't lost his very thick accent; and he keeps to himself. Lives alone, I'm pretty sure. He certainly isn't married, as far as I know. Works in a car plant. Donates regularly to the parish. Not much else, sorry to say. Why?"

"She's worried about him. That is, she's worried about the interactions between him and her mother. And now, in the light of her mother's death, she's suspicious of him."

"Really! She going to do anything: tell the police or try talking to him?"

"She didn't mention talking to him. I hope she doesn't try that. As to the police, the thought has crossed her mind. But I think I talked her into putting that on hold 'til the autopsy's available."

"Smart thinking. You convinced she'll do that – wait, I mean?"

"Pretty much so, yes. I was just hoping you might be able to shed light on the possibility of his being a threat. She described some rowdy confrontations between the two of them, mostly on the man's part. Think he's capable of physical violence? There's been none so far, according to the daughter, just verbal theatrics."

"I doubt it – no reports of anything like that so far. He's blustery, but I chalk that up to being an immigrant in a foreign culture. And living alone like that, he probably doesn't get enough feedback to really learn the nuances he ought to know about. My guess is he's defensive and protects himself with aggression. And he probably does that without a second thought on the matter. I'm guessing it's just an intuitional thing – maybe fits his personality as well. But, I must say, I've not even had a conversation with the man. I just hear things, you know – pastoral ear to the ground."

"What you say makes sense. Well," John said, rising from his chair, "I told her to wait and I hope she does. She ought to hear back from the medical folks today."

"Keep me in the loop, John."

"I will. That's more or less what I asked of the daughter – to keep me informed. Talk to you later," he said, and turned toward the door. But before he left the room, he turned. "Be sure to let me know if there are any calls, okay?"

"Sure enough. You might want to tell the receptionist too."

"Right." Father John ambled over to her office and did just that.

Time dragged on slowly over the next hour or so. Father John was beginning to lose hope that Michael would call when the receptionist buzzed him to pick up line one. By then he was half-expecting it to be Algoma and made a mental note to call them if it wasn't. They needed to be kept abreast of his travel situation.

"Hello?"

"Father John?" It was Michael.

Thank God! Let's hope he wants to talk. "Yes. Is that you, Michael?"

"It is." The voice didn't sound warm, but at least he had called.

"How do you feel this morning?" Father John didn't quite know how to get into the heart of things without scaring him off again and decided to ease into the conversation.

"I'm okay now. Maybe we could get together again."

"I'd like that, Michael. What do you have in mind? I mean, when would you like to do it? And where?"

"I could come this afternoon. Right after lunch, okay?"

"That works. Here at the rectory?"

"That's what I had in mind."

"Well, then, I'll see you here around one. Thanks again for reconsidering."

"Goodbye." And Michael was gone without further fanfare.

That's a relief! Be careful this time, John. Don't want to lose him again – whatever it was that drove him off.

CHAPTER VIII – EPIPHANY

Father John greeted Michael at the front door. But instead of following the priest up the several stairs to the office, he pointedly stopped inside the door and after greeting him said: "On my way here, I rethought the idea about talking here. I think I'd rather like to go to a restaurant again. But perhaps a different one, if you don't mind."

"That works for me. I'll have to get my coat."

"I'll be outside. I left the engine running."

"I'll only be a moment," Father John said, and let Michael outside again. He then turned to head upstairs for his coat. On the way back, he popped his head into the receptionist's office to say he'd be out for a while. "I don't know how long. So would you take calls for me?"

"Sure, Father. Have fun."

He smiled in return and stepped out into the cold early afternoon air. *The weather's not really any better. Hope I can get out of here sometime soon.*

They ended up at a small coffee shop and again got a small table in the rear. The lunch crowd, such as it might have been, had obviously evaporated and they had the place literally to themselves. Father John waited for Michael to resume their conversation.

After the coffee they'd ordered appeared, Michael finally spoke. "I'm sorry for the delay, Father, but this is a very emotional time for me. I think I can continue today. But this story of mine is so complicated that I think you have to hear it with all its pieces in the right place, so, pardon me for asking, but exactly where was I? I think I'd just told you Irene had thought – had feared, really – that I had come for more than just completing the story of Dad's war record. Is that where I was?"

"Yes, Michael, it was," Father John said.

"Well then, that's what she said. She thought I might have come for some other purpose.

"'Like what?' I asked, genuinely puzzled.

"'Well, you see … ' She was dragging her words out, apparently speaking very carefully. 'I not only knew of your father, but I also knew about you. I'd seen you as a baby, in fact.'

"Stunned, I was unsure what to say next. 'You mean, you actually met my parents and saw me? Or what? You worked at the adoption agency?'

"'No, I didn't work for them. But I did see you as a little baby.'

"Now I was totally at sea and, not knowing what to say, just sat there. And I kept staring at the woman.

"'I don't know how to say this, Michael, so I'll just launch into it, okay? Pat and I didn't marry 'til after the war. Your parents too, right?'

"I nodded silently in the affirmative.

"'Well, I was so caught up by the war that I had volunteered at the USO while I was waiting for Pat. We were very much in love and I wanted him so much,' she said, stretching out the adverb.

"'But with his hitch in the service beginning to lengthen because of the way the war was going, and with the reports sounding daily more grim, my moods began to bounce up and down like a yo-yo. I went from planning our time together when he returned to feeling like he wasn't going to be coming back. And all this time I was working full-time as well as volunteering many evenings at the USO.

"'I don't think it was strictly by the books, but our canteen accepted not only actual servicemen, but draftees before they shipped out to training – even boys who said they were planning to enlist soon. I imagine a number of those might not have actually gone into service. But what the hell, it was a place to meet girls. And some girls were as lonely as they were. Well, one night I met your father there.'

"My jaw must have dropped noticeably, but I remained silent.

"'Yeah, figure the odds,' she said in response to the look on my face. 'He kept coming back. And I guess I was in one of my moods: feeling sorry for myself, imagining that Pat wouldn't be coming back. No one there knew about Pat and me, you see. I wasn't wearing the ring he gave me when we got engaged before he left. We were all told not to wear wedding or engagement rings and also not to get attached to anybody we met at the canteen. We shouldn't give out addresses or phone numbers, either. No connections. Ordinarily that wasn't a problem, because we wouldn't see the guys much before they'd have to be going to another base or overseas. Besides, most of us were only there a couple nights a week anyway.

"'But Walter's case was different. He was allowed more time after signing up because of his mother. She was recovering from surgery, and Walter took care of her days while he was working at a garage near their home – and his employers allowed him to check on her at lunch and over breaks. Besides, his job was only part-time. Evenings, his dad was home, so Walter could get away, and he usually came to the USO, especially after we hooked up. So he ended up with some extra weeks before Basic ... and we got to know each other more than canteen officials would have wanted.

"'I never told Walter about my engagement. I figured that, like the rest, he'd be gone soon – soon enough, anyway – and I'd sort out my feelings then. And, besides, maybe Pat might not be coming back, after all. The logic was complicated, and not all that square, but I'm just telling you the way it actually was.

"'I didn't bank on getting carried away, really I didn't. It was all so morally ambiguous. Later I couldn't believe I'd gotten that involved. Well, anyway, I did something Pat and I never did: I slept with your Dad. Not just once, but two or three times. I felt so guilty afterward, but I couldn't help myself at the time. I think he felt that way too. Well, that's what happened.

"'When his time for Basic Training finally came, I was tearful. We promised to write, but in my heart I think I was fairly certain I wouldn't be doing that. Sure enough, your dad's letters started coming from Basic, and then California before he shipped out, even a few from Korea. I never answered them, and after a while I even stopped opening them. I threw them all away.

"'I began working through it in my own way, eventually rationalizing that while I shouldn't have slept with him like that, it wasn't a real commitment and I shouldn't honor it. I should honor the commitment to Pat instead, and I began hoping again he'd make it back. I even started dreaming about the kind of wedding we could have.

"'When your dad got to Korea, it was a couple of months after we'd met, and his letters finally stopped altogether. I didn't know how he was handling our involvement and don't know to this day. I can only imagine that he did get over it and that his marriage was as genuine as anybody would want. I know that I was able to get past it and was again centered on Pat.'

"She looked at me for a long time. 'This has to be troubling for you. And I want to apologize to you ... and, in a way, to your dad, too. I was foolish. I can say today that I shouldn't have done it. But there it is: I did do it ... and I'm so very sorry.

"'But,' she said after a slight pause, and she drew out the word, just as she had earlier, 'it didn't end there. Pat had been writing too, of course, and I was answering his letters. But about three months after Walter and I had parted, I became conflicted about writing to Pat – because I began to suspect I was pregnant. And soon a doctor confirmed that I was.'

"She stopped, to allow me to put myself together and perhaps respond. But whatever I was thinking, I kept my silence – and my stare, which was steadily intensifying. She could see from my face that what she'd just said was registering, and in all probability, uncomfortably.

"So she slowly and reluctantly continued. 'I needed a plan, and quickly. I told my parents that there were better jobs in Rockford and I was going there to get one. It would be difficult to get back and forth from there, but I would stay in touch by mail and phone. So I quit my job and left.

"'It wasn't an easy time, you can imagine, but I got help through the church in Rockford: part-time work for as long as I was physically able to do it, plus residence in a home for "unwed mothers," as they used to say. All that was set up before I told my parents, of course. I was determined to have the child, and when I did six months later, I immediately offered it for adoption. I never told Pat or my parents – or your father, either. I thought that would end it. I earnestly hoped so, anyway.

"'And I continued writing Pat – how could I not? What I told him was that I was working in Rockford, and I mentioned absolutely nothing about the child. More and more I wanted to be with him and be married to him. While I had sinned against him, I hoped he'd never find out.

"'A priest there told me, in fact, that I didn't have to tell, that it would be better if I didn't – as long as I really did love Pat and intended to marry him, which was true. I was relieved to hear that from the priest, of course. And I made a very sincere confession – early in my pregnancy, in fact – plus several more before the birth, just to be sure.

"'Once the boy was in the adoption process, I made up the rest of the story for my parents and Pat: I was coming back because the job had run its course and I hadn't made that much money after all. And I said how much I longed for Pat's return. All that stuff about my feelings was surely true. At least that part was true and sincere.'

"Her face had grown increasingly serious and sad, and she paused again. I felt drained but continued to hold my tongue. So Irene once more picked up the thread of her narrative.

"'I didn't learn about your dad's war-time connection with Pat 'til after Pat returned home. I couldn't believe it. What are the odds of that? Naturally, I continued to keep silent about him. But when Pat explained the medal thing, I really felt at odds. I wanted him to do the right thing by your father, but I sure didn't want to see Walter again. And if it came to that, if the two war buddies were to get together again, I'd figure something out. I'd have to. Well, as you know, I didn't have to. But for the longest time I agonized over even the possibility of that happening.

"'Within several months of Pat's return, then, we had that wedding I'd dreamed of, though not nearly as elaborate as I'd fantasized. And we began married life. In time the two kids came, and your dad was completely gone from my mind. Pat and I were really happy with each other and with the children. Your dad and my fling with him – it was adolescent of me, even if I was out of my teens – were completely out of my mind.'

"She paused again, and I probably looked like I was about to say something like *I don't need to hear this*. But I didn't say anything, and Irene continued.

"'But then ... perhaps twelve years into my marriage, I began to get curious about that first baby of mine. I don't know what prompted the feelings, but something did. I mean, after all, I'd already had two children with Pat – it wasn't like my maternal instincts were starved or anything. But it became like an obsession. And I couldn't shake it.

"'I couldn't let on to Pat, of course, so I discreetly contacted Rockford Catholic Charities on my own. Some of the same people were still there, and once they looked up my case, they said they remembered me. I don't know if they really did, but they said so. Anyway, they said the baby had gotten a wonderful home, but they weren't permitted to divulge any other information – not a word. I'd hit a dead end, and so I resigned myself to at least knowing that my child was with good and loving people.

"'But the gnawing need to know wouldn't go away. A few months later I got the bright idea of looking up the priest who'd helped me at the time, and when I was able to finally reach him, we had a long phone conversation. I guess he felt sorry for me. He'd make inquiries, he said. It took several more months, but he finally called one day while Pat was at work.

"'This time we had a very long conversation. He wanted to be sure that I wouldn't make a scene – or, worse, sue somebody. When he finally told me the family's name – just their name, no address or anything else, mind you – I was floored. He said *Mr. and Mrs. Walter Partland.*'

"My look was now clearly one of incomprehension, or agitation. I don't think Irene could be sure. But she continued, nonetheless. 'The priest had to have known from my reaction that something was wrong. I may have gasped or something. There was certainly a long gap in the conversation on my end. He asked if I was okay. When I got my wits back, of course I said that I was fine. I lied. *All I really want is my baby's last name, and to be reassured that he was in a good home – and a Catholic one. He is Catholic, isn't he, Father? It's a little overwhelming for me right now.*

"'I assured him I wouldn't try to see the child or the family. And I certainly didn't want to bring suit. Of course, I wouldn't do that. How could I have even dared, had I wanted to? And I surely didn't want to.

"'I thanked him, and the conversation didn't last much longer. He was reassured when we hung up, I believe. But I was a mess. You had ended up with your true father. I just couldn't believe it all. Twice it happened that astronomical odds slapped me square in the face. Unbelievable!

"'And now, you show up here today. I didn't even know your first name 'til now. And may I say it now? You really look like your father, at least as I remember him as a young man back then. Perhaps others have told you that? Anyway, I thought for sure you were looking for your birth mother – what else could it possibly be? I got very scared. I can't imagine you didn't notice. But after we talked and it became clear you had no clue about any of that, I relaxed. And yet, the more we talked, the more the old feelings started to kick in again. I mean, seeing my own son all grown up and everything. You can't imagine how I've been feeling since you knocked on my door this afternoon.

"'And I need to tell you: now that we've finally met, I have very quickly come to like you, Michael – a lot. Your devotion to your father, your sincerity, your polite demeanor – it's all so beautiful. And over supper, I was torn between telling you everything and letting you walk away, probably forever. By now you can see how I solved that dilemma. I want you in my life.

"'Michael, I'm your mother, and I'm so grateful that I have been allowed to meet you as a grown man. You can't imagine how often you've been in my thoughts and how often I've wondered what you might be like. But never in my wildest dreams did I even consider it possible that I would actually meet you some day. It was just one of those fantasies mothers have, I suppose.

"'But now that it has come true, now that you've actually walked into my life … from what I've learned in this short time, I could not have asked for a nicer son.'"

"She smiled, sweetly, and then looked at me long and soulfully, Father. And then she said 'I only hope you don't hate me for all this.'"

CHAPTER IX – DEJA VU

The silence that now descended upon the two in the restaurant jarred Father John out of the story and back into real time. Michael was again near tears, and the priest momentarily didn't know what to say.

The younger man had stopped talking and was choking back his emotions and trying to compose himself. Finally he looked at the priest. "She looked so pathetic, so earnest, Father. You can't imagine …"

Father John thought he could guess but didn't say so. He felt as though he had been in the room with the two of them, a privileged voyeur, and he believed he'd been feeling some of the things they had felt. He finally broke the silence. "Do you, Michael … hate her?"

Looking pained, Michael responded: "Of course not, Father. Why would you ask that?"

"Well, she asked you, and you didn't reply to her, at least not so far as you've indicated so far. And forgive my saying it, but she's dead now, and I'm reasonably sure you know that. I'm also reasonably sure you know, and as I've suspected and, for all I know, the police may too, she didn't die outside church. And you asked to go to confession."

The look that came over Michael at that moment was one of sheer panic. "I thought I could trust you. But you and the police …

Are you spying for them?" His tone had turned instantly very cold, as had the stare that he fixed on the priest.

Father John, in turn, realized that his ability to help, to patch up this hurting soul, was suddenly and seriously in jeopardy. His response sounded lame, even to himself: "Michael, please, I'm here as a priest, not as some police spy."

But the younger man was having none of it. And before Father John could say anything else, Michael silently took out a few bills from his wallet, laid them on the table and rose. "The cab's leaving. If you don't want to end up walking, you'd best move now." And with that he made for the front door.

Father John gathered his coat as quickly as he could and hurried after the younger man, worried less about his ride than about restoring the trust that was so suddenly and apparently completely evaporating into thin air. The was the second time their attempts at confession had been interrupted, and however innocent Father John felt about the first time, he was absolutely sure he was to blame for this second one.

He had barely time to get to the car before the engine roared to life and they were heading carefully back to the rectory, Michael with his eyes silently and stoically fixed on the road ahead. Father John tried several times to enlist a response from him, but got not a word from the younger man.

When they arrived at the rectory's front door, Father John asked if Michael would call him later. "I see how upset you are, but I'd like a chance to talk this through, Michael. And I believe, and hope, that in a little while you'll be of a mind to try that. Please," he said, drawing out the word, "if I can't persuade you to stay, at least call me tonight."

But Michael's eyes never flickered. And when the disheartened priest finally shut the door, the car moved forward immediately, its driver never so much as glancing sideways at the priest.

Father John stood there in the cold, feeling terrible, confused and defeated. *How did I let that happen? Of all the inept and insensitive moves!* Nothing he could think or say to himself could console him, and his mind immediately became a jumble of what-ifs, of possibilities seemingly stacked up in the ether and waiting to jump into reality, and any of them would complicate things beyond imagining.

He was suddenly aware of how dark it had become. How had he missed that at the restaurant? He'd been facing the front of the restaurant, but apparently was too engrossed in Michael's tale to notice. The enveloping darkness was ominous, an almost tangible version of what he was feeling inside. But as inconsolable as he felt, he was more concerned about Michael. *He had wanted confession. And not only doesn't he have God's forgiveness now, or the church's, but he may also not seek it again!* And John Henry Wintermann placed the blame for that securely on his own sagging, aging shoulders.

Sleep was not about to come easily, even had he not determined to wait up as long as it took for the call he so desperately hoped would be coming from Michael. But it might well not come, he knew, and knowing that and being resigned to it were two different things.

He went slowly into the rectory and briefly plucked David, the teenager in the office, away from the TV program that helped him pass the time. He told him to be absolutely sure to find him if any call came for him, and to be just as sure to let him know when he was leaving for the evening so he could then be on the lookout for calls himself.

Satisfied that the young fellow understood him, Father John trudged up the stairs to his room to find his breviary. If he could do nothing else, he hoped he could at least pray: for Michael ... and for all inept clerics, wherever they may find themselves on this cold, dark night.

CHAPTER X – ROAD REPAIR

He finished his prayers and placed the breviary on his nightstand. He rose and stretched, and then looked at the time. It was barely past six o'clock: probably too soon to hope Michael had changed his mind about calling, given the roads and the extra time it must be taking for him to drive to his South Side home.

He went looking for Bill. The high school student downstairs indicated that he was out. That was all he volunteered, perhaps not knowing any more than that. So John went into the kitchen in search of something. Not very pleased with the possibilities, he opted for a piece of toast and a cup of tea with honey, all of which he took upstairs to the common room.

But instead of sitting in front of the TV, he went to the table at the other end of the room to ponder things as he slowly sipped his tea. The honey was a nice touch, he decided, but he quickly moved his mind into thinking about Michael.

He had come to like him a lot in the rather brief time they'd been together – all the more reason to be downhearted at this turn of events. He found his almost-transparent sincerity quite endearing. And then it struck him. *If I've seen that correctly, that's the key. Michael couldn't have done it, couldn't have murdered her. Whatever he did, whatever is on his mind to confess, it can't be murder.*

That didn't help him feel any better, he realized, but it gave him some clarity that had been eluding him since Michael walked out of the restaurant. He hoped all the more now that Michael would call. He wasn't sure how he'd convince him, but he knew he'd try like the devil to have him understand that he really had good reason to trust him. Forget his being a priest; forget the seal of confession; forget all that church stuff. John Henry Wintermann now understood in his deepest being that Michael was innocent of the woman's death. He knew it; he felt it. In the only court that mattered to him, Father John knew in his own mind that Michael Partland was innocent. *That's what I have to get across to him – and I swear I will. If only he calls!*

He prayed again for the lad. *Interesting! He's not really that young, but somehow to me he's like a babe in the woods. And he needs my prayers.* So Father John lost himself in praying for Michael and didn't even realize his negative feelings had disappeared, or at very least that he was no longer aware of them.

When he became aware again of his surroundings, he was surprised that it was closing in on seven o'clock. He roused himself and went downstairs to check with the young man in the office. No calls had come – none for him or Father Bill or anybody – and Father Bill wasn't back, either. So Father John wandered back upstairs. *If only I could call him – but I don't have his number or address. But wait a minute! Perhaps I can call anyway. He lives on the South Side. Maybe the young man downstairs can find that in the phone book. I don't know his mom's first name – let's hope the listing is still in his dad's name.*

In no time the teen had found a South Side listing for a Walter Partland, and Father John moved to the next office, closed the door and sat down to try it. But he spent some time in thought before picking up the receiver. He punched in the numbers very slowly and deliberately.

"Hello," said a woman's voice on the other end.

"Is this the Partland residence?"

"Yes."

"May I speak with Michael, please?"

"Just a moment," she said, and put the receiver down.

Shortly Michael's voice came over the phone: "Hello?"

"Michael, this is Father Wintermann. Please don't put the phone down. Just listen for a moment. Will you do that, please?"

There was no answer, but Father John could tell that the connection hadn't been broken, so he continued. "I don't know if you've had enough time to think since you dropped me off, but I have. And there's something I need to say, aside from apologizing again for having turned you off – and this time I'm sure I'm guilty of that. I hope you can forgive me. But what I have to say is this: I admit your request for confession along with Mrs. O'Carroll's death had me believing you were somehow responsible for that and wanted forgiveness for it. But since leaving you, I've come to realize you couldn't possibly have killed her."

There was still a maddening silence on Michael's end, but Father John waited. He'd said what he needed to, at least the gist of it, and was willing to give the young man time to process that.

At last Michael responded. "And just how do you figure that?"

"Your sincerity and the obvious joy you exhibited at finding your own mother. Those came across clearly to me. And someone like that couldn't have murdered the source of all that joy."

Again, silence. And then: "How'd you find me?"

"Walter Partland's listed in the phone book."

"Oh." More silence.

Finally, Father John could take it no longer. He had to say something. "Well? Am I right?"

"What if you are?"

"Am I?"

"Yes ... I didn't do that." He sounded guarded, like he perhaps didn't want his mother to hear anything.

"But you're still unwilling to talk further?"

"I didn't say that."

Don't act like a petulant little kid, Michael. "Can we talk?"

"Tonight?"

"If you like." And when Michael didn't respond, he added: "Or tomorrow, if it's too late already."

"I'm not sure."

"Michael, I can help you. You wanted confession. Let me do that for you. Please."

"I'll think about it. Overnight."

"Will you call me tomorrow, then? Please."

"Probably." And after a slight pause, he said: "Goodnight." And then, in what sounded like an afterthought he said: "Thank you for calling." Then he hung up.

Not sure exactly where things stood, Father John at last decided that the final thank you probably meant Michael would call in the morning. He hoped so. And buoyed by that, he felt he'd be able to sleep after all. So he went to his room to try out that theory.

But before he could even undress, the intercom sounded and the high school student informed him that someone was on the line for him.

"Hello," he said tentatively.

It was Michael. "I decided that I couldn't wait. I'll take you up on your offer."

"You'd like to talk tonight?" He tried not to sound incredulous.

"Yes. I can leave right now."

"I'll be expecting you here. Should I have my coat ready?"

"Yes," was all he said before hanging up.

An hour or so later, Father John found himself once again in Michael's car. "It's still pretty cold out, Michael. I could easily see my breath just now." *Pretty lame small talk, John.*

"Yes, but the weather report promises some warming tomorrow – enough that the ice should start to melt, I think." Michael didn't seem hostile, but he wasn't very outgoing, either.

Good news! I'll be able to drive back soon. Don't think I'll mention that just now, though. "Hope so. I'm not used to this much cold, and these dangerous streets aren't to my liking, either."

"Yeah, and you should be able to get back in time for Christmas, too." Michael had maybe read his mind.

"That too. But first, thanks for coming. I hope I can finally hear your confession. I can't tell you how happy and relieved I am to see you."

Michael didn't react to his apology. Instead, he suggested the same restaurant they'd first gone to, perhaps because he knew it would be open late. They were soon sipping from steaming mugs: coffee for Michael and tea for Father John, who decided to stay with what he'd had back at St. Hilary's. In very business-like fashion, Michael said: "Where was I? I think I'd finished telling you about hearing Mrs. O'Carroll's – Mom's – story and learning of our connections."

"I'm sure that's right." Father John was watching him closely. *Maybe he's simply taking his good old sweet time getting over his anger. Or maybe he's sniffing me out, making sure I really meant it when I said I was an insensitive clod and am sorry about it.*

"When it finally came time for me to respond …" Michael was continuing, "or, should I say, when I was finally able to respond … I got up and went to her, lifted her up out of her chair, and we got lost in a long embrace. I was crying. I think she was too. No. I'm sure she was. I don't know how long that lasted, but a long time. No words – just that hug. God, it felt so good!

"When it was finally over and we backed away from each other, I sat down next to her, on the end of the couch. And we talked about all the things we could only guess at: like how she handled the separation from her child – from me – and how I'd gotten along in the Partland family. You know, lots of things like that.

"She told me how very important it was when she was finally able to talk to the people in Rockford and how disappointed she was when they couldn't – wouldn't – give her any information. She told me how scared she became when she learned that Pat and Dad had been Army buddies and might get together again – that is, if Pat ever pursued the medal thing."

The more the younger man talked, the more Father John felt his intuition had been correct. *He simply can't have killed his own mother.*

Michael was continuing, more and more wrapped up in his tale: "We must have talked for at least another hour, and it felt so good, Father. Then she showed me what else she had in her Bible: my birth certificate! I didn't wonder at the time, but I did later, whether she put that in there only after Pat's death. It seems it wouldn't be too smart to keep it there before then. But at the moment, I didn't question it. I was just so happy to see it. And she told me I could have that too.

"We had another cup of coffee and just kept talking. I wished it didn't have to end. But eventually I had to go back to the South Side. Before I went, however, we discussed how much of this I should share with my Mom. I mean – you know – the one on the South Side. Anyway, we agreed on telling her everything, and that's what I was going to do."

Michael's face started to change. It wasn't immediately clear to Father John what was happening, but he soon figured out that what the younger man was moving into was affecting him deeply. Michael's eyes narrowed, his speech slowed down, and the twitch was back in his hand. And he looked more narrowly focused, more intense.

"I finally got up to gather my things over by the door. And when I turned around to kiss her goodbye, she was getting up from her chair. And the next thing I knew, she was falling forward. She cracked her head something fierce on the Bible, of all things, there on the coffee table. The noise was terrible and startling – like a gunshot. And then she didn't move. It was awful. She must have caught her shoe on the rug or something. But there she was on the floor.

"I was so startled that I couldn't do anything for a couple of seconds. By the time I got my wits about me, I went right to her. But she wasn't moving. And when I tried to find one, there was no pulse.

"And then I panicked. I didn't know what to do. My first thought was 911. But then I realized two things almost at once. She was obviously dead – there was no pulse – so what good was calling the police? I didn't even think of CPR, though I'm convinced now that it wouldn't have helped.

"And second, how would I explain all this? I'd have to say what I was there for – about Dad and all. But I'm sure the cops would want to see everything, and they'd see the birth certificate and Walter's letter. I began to imagine that they would suspect that I was there to blackmail her or to extort money. And maybe even they'd claim that I pushed her when she wouldn't pay. My mind was racing in lots of directions, and what it was dredging up – none of it – sounded very good for me. So I didn't call the police.

"But then I had to figure out what I should do. I had no good ideas. I was worried now how much to tell Mom when I got back home. I eventually decided that I shouldn't go home that night. I called the South Side with a made-up story – and not a very good one, I think, but Mom bought it – about why I wouldn't be home that night, and that I'd see her the next day."

Father John was feeling Michael's confusion and sadness, and he kept listening eagerly, his eyes fixed on the younger man's face.

"But at that point I still didn't know what to do about Irene. It eventually came to me that I should bring her to church and make it look like she fell trying to go to mass. It sounded good at the time. She's Catholic, right? And she surely goes to mass, right? So that's what I finally decided.

"I had to wait most of what turned out to be a very long night. I had the presence of mind to dress her in her coat more or less as soon as I'd hatched my plan, and I added her purse, which I found in her bedroom.

"She was already stretched out where she fell, so after I finally got the coat on, I put her back the same way. I had no idea how difficult it was to dress someone like that. But I remembered hearing somewhere that rigor mortis would set in and it would kind of freeze the body into the position it had at death. I figured I had time for a little leeway once I decided to put the coat on her, and I tried to keep her elongated like she was on her front-room floor. As upset as I was, I'm surprised I could think this much through.

"I waited 'til after four o'clock. But I hadn't bargained on all that ice. I was so disturbed, I guess, that I didn't notice it happening, and I still don't know when exactly it did. Maybe those things occur quietly, I don't know. But I sure didn't catch it. So when I went outside to ready the car, I was shocked at the state of things out there.

"I was able to get her into the car all right because I was in the driveway next to her home and just pulled the car quietly to her back door. I put her lengthwise into the back seat, her legs draping over the seat onto the floor just a little bit. She barely fit, and while it wasn't easy, I got it to happen."

He paused for a quick breath, looked around, but kept going after that quick gulp of air. "I was lucky it was so dark. And I was pretty quiet, too. No one saw me put her into the car, I'm pretty sure. I had to drive slow and careful over those couple of blocks to the church. And I got lucky again over there, because there wasn't any light at all in the lot between school and the rectory.

"I had parked there for the funeral because my Mom knew about that space. And I figured that it was protected enough that I could drive right up to the church door and move her out without being seen, even if it was lit up. But for some reason it wasn't. I'd already figured that if there were lights in any of the apartments across Fairfield, I'd have to come back later – they're the only ones who could possibly see anything going on in that lot. But the apartments were dark, and I drove right in. Once I was able to judge the distance, I cut my headlights and eased up to the side door.

"It was pretty slick there and I had a dickens of a time getting her out and then positioning her just right at the church door. It finally looked to me like most people would figure she slipped coming to early mass, hit her head and died. I got out of there quietly and went looking for a motel out of the immediate area for at least a few hours of sleep – more like rest, because I didn't really sleep.

"Later in the morning I went back home and worried about things before I thought to call you and try to talk about this. Mom bought my story from the night before, but I was a mess, and the only way I could hide that was to stay in my room 'til I left for your place. I really took a chance because I didn't call you 'til I got on my way. I didn't want Mom to overhear a thing."

Michael stopped as if searching for what to say next or how to say it, and Father John finally got a word in edgewise. He figured that this far into the story, Michael was probably over his snit. But he was still going to be careful. "How'd you square things at work? Taking the day of the funeral was easy, I suppose. But today?"

"Oh, I had some days coming and I just took them for Christmas. No big deal there. I'm using more besides – all the way to Christmas."

"Help me out a bit. You mentioned confession. Pardon me, but, as I've told you, I had thought you had a hand in her death. But I've finally concluded – and your story today validates my conclusions – that's not the case. So I'm confused about what you need to confess, Michael."

"Father," Michael said slowly, seemingly near exasperation with either his inability to communicate or the priest's to understand … or both. "I suspect what I did is at least highly illegal. Besides, I think I was somehow involved in her death after all."

"It may or may not be illegal, Michael," Father John said, picking his words carefully, "I'll get back to that. But as to the other thing: How do you think you had something sinful to do with her death? I'll grant you, the whole thing is traumatic and all, but sinful involvement? I don't see it. Help me here."

"She wouldn't have been in that situation if I hadn't come along, Father. I figure at the end there she was so eager to get to me to hug or kiss me goodbye that she hurried and didn't watch properly … "

"Slow down, slow down," the priest said. "Now you're putting two and two together and getting five. Do I need to go into the difference between the cause of sin and an occasion of sin?" He thought he had that right, but on reflection wasn't sure. In any event, he was surprised how quickly that had popped into his mind more than forty years after seminary Moral Class. It was something like that, he knew.

"What?" Michael asked, genuinely perplexed.

"What I'm getting at is this: sin must be willed, Michael. It's not just a peculiar bunching together of possibilities, such as in your case. You no more willed your mother's death than I did. You didn't cause her to die. At least, so it seems to me – not from what you've said. Anyway, there are other things we should look at. Did she say anything before she fell – or as she fell?"

"Why?"

"Never mind, just tell me. Did she?"

"I don't remember."

"Think. Take your time." Father John waited while Michael hesitated and finally started genuinely searching his memory.

Finally he said, pain etched into his face: "I just can't be sure."

"Try some more. Please."

After a rather long time he said: "She may have uttered a sound … like *oh,* or something."

"May have?"

"The more I think of it, something like that escaped her lips. I'm pretty sure it was 'oh.' But it was drawn out like this: 'oooh.' But what does that prove?"

"Well, it may mean that something was happening to her other than the falling, and that she was aware of it – at the last moment, so to speak."

"So?"

"So she may have died of something natural: a heart attack, a stroke, an aneurysm – things like that. And if so, all the more reason for you not to blame yourself. And a court wouldn't blame you, it should go without saying."

Michael looked as if he were beginning to see what the priest was getting at, and beginning to see light at the end of his private tunnel.

"Now, as to moving the body … " the priest continued. And Michael's face fell again. "Hold on," Father John said, seeing his reaction. "Let me finish. I don't know what the police might say about that. If – if, I say – a court were to determine you had some hand in causing her death, then moving her body would certainly be a further legal problem, with further legal ramifications. But you didn't, so far as I can see, either legally or morally, have anything to do with causing her to die. At most, I imagine the police wouldn't like what you did, moving her body like that, but of itself I just don't think it's any kind of crime. But more to the point here, it's not something you should consider mortally sinful.

"You shouldn't have done it, I suppose. But that's a far cry from calling it a sin – and maybe from calling it a crime too, for all I know. I'm not a lawyer. If it becomes important to find that out, we can ask someone to educate us. Again I say: if!

"You see, Michael, there are all sorts of issues here, and we need to consider them one at a time." The look on Michael's face caused him to stop. "What is it?" Father John asked gently.

"You're going too fast, Father. Slow down and back up."

"Okay. Where should I go to help make sense of this for you?"

"You're talking legal and moral. How about there?"

"Okay. Courts and the police are concerned with legal stuff. Confession deals with morality. So far so good?"

"Yeah."

"The two don't necessarily coincide. In fact, they often don't. To use a silly example, it's a crime to spit on the sidewalk. Actually that came from the flu epidemic early in the last century and was a pretty good idea at the time. You'd be surprised, perhaps, to learn that lots of men at that time didn't use handkerchiefs to blow their noses. They just blew stuff out onto the ground ... or the sidewalk. Things like that and sneezing could contribute to spreading the flu. So they outlawed "spitting." After only a few years, the epidemic was over and forgotten, and the law was rarely enforced, eventually becoming the subject of lots of humor. But it was a good idea originally.

"Once the epidemic was over, spitting on a sidewalk was not threatening anyone's health and it was no longer a moral concern, either. After all, to deliberately spread disease is a moral issue, right? But years later there was no longer a moral dimension to spitting on sidewalks.

"So the next question then is: is it still illegal? Technically, yes – but not easily enforceable or enforced. By now it's pretty much small potatoes. See the difference? Or, at least, can you see how there can be a difference?"

"Yes, I think so."

"Well, then, so far as your confession goes, we're not concerned with civil legalities but with all those things you probably learned about sin in the catechism: serious matter – that is, something morally wrong and serious enough to maybe amount to sin; proper awareness and proper decision on the part of someone; and, especially, a truly free choice. Again, so far so good?"

"Yes," Michael said slowly, a very faint light starting to show behind his eyeballs.

"In your case, Irene's death is serious, all right. But I don't see where you wanted it to happen, let alone that you freely and deliberately caused it."

Michael looked relieved and smiled, sheepishly. "I guess you may be right. I surely didn't want her to die. And I didn't push her or anything like that. But whenever I thought about it before now, I'd just get overwhelmed over being present when she died like that … and it made me feel guilty."

"Well, I hope you can see now, with a little reflection, that you needn't feel that way because there's nothing sinful there – not so far as I can see, anyway. Can you agree?"

"I think so," Michael said slowly.

"But it's taking a while to adjust to it?"

"Yes," he said more quickly.

"Well, take all the time you need. But while you are, can we discuss the legal stuff?"

CHAPTER XI – CONFESSION

"What?" Michael said, just as the waitress came to check on them. So he waited 'til after she returned with more tea and coffee, and then repeated: "What? Legal stuff?"

"As I said, I'm no lawyer, but moving a dead body might qualify as legally discussable. If ... "

"If what?"

"If the police find out about it," the priest said, coyly.

"What do you mean "if?" They'll want to know, won't they? And we should tell, no?"

"Maybe not. Let's talk about that a moment." And when Michael looked genuinely perplexed again, he added: "Perhaps I need to talk about the seal of confession."

The puzzled look on Michael's face didn't change.

"You know about that, at least in general, right?"

"Priests can't tell what they hear in confession. Correct?" But Michael looked as if he didn't know where this was heading.

"Very good! But you may not know it also applies to anyone who overhears a confession. Such people may not talk, either. Actually, only penitents are free to talk about confessional matters – because it's their stuff, right? So a priest may discuss such things only with a penitent's permission. That's to ensure trust in the process, no doubt, but also and especially to protect reputations. Even sinners have a right to their good names. Got it, so far?"

"Yeah. Though I didn't know about others not being allowed to talk. But it makes sense. So what's that got to do with me? You trying to reassure me I can trust you? Or what?"

"No. Rather, this: I can't tell the police anything I've heard here unless you give permission. And I can't force you to give it to me. In fact, I'm going to insist that you don't let me talk to the police."

"Wait a minute, Father. I haven't confessed yet. So there's nothing stopping you."

"But the church takes things like that into consideration too. Once a conversation begins that's even thought to be a confession or maybe is barely the beginnings of one, those things fall under the seal too. *Putative* confessions, they're called. Roughly, that's "thought-to-be confessions," which is awkward in English, but not in Latin. So my seminary teacher said when we students giggled about the translation. Maybe "presumed" confessions is better.

"Anyway, I can't talk about any of this without your go-ahead. And the significance of that, Michael," he said, drawing out his words, "is that the police may not know enough to ask the pertinent questions. They certainly haven't written their report about finding Irene's body with that in mind – not so far as I know, anyway. It has Irene dying where they found the body: outside church. And while I suspected otherwise, I didn't let on at the time. And I'm not going to, either. That would be my stance even if you and I never talked. But especially now that we have, I certainly won't be saying anything. And, more to the point, I think you shouldn't either."

Michael's face betrayed his lack of understanding. "Why not? Wouldn't a lawyer tell me to? Wouldn't the police want to know that?"

"I don't know if they would, Michael. But I'm pretty sure a lawyer would tell you not to volunteer anything like that. But there are other, non-legal, reasons why you shouldn't tell them. The explanation may sound complicated, but ... bottom line: I don't see a need to.

"See, you're not guilty of any sin here, not that I can see. And as to legalities, there's been no murder, no crime. Unless some other good is served by your telling or some other harm is averted or rectified by that, I don't see why you should speak up.

"Now, it does remain to be discovered what Irene's family may want or need to know about all this. And as it turns out, I think I can help find that out without revealing confessional secrets. Are you willing to allow me that – a chat with Irene's family ... without giving away anything, including the fact that we've even spoken together?"

Michael wasn't sure what to say. "I guess ... but can we talk about it some more, maybe? At least a little?"

"Sure – as much as you want."

"You say you can talk with Irene's family without revealing anything I've told you? How? They're going to know you're on to something, aren't they?"

"I think I can avoid that."

"That's hard to believe, Father. Once you broach the subject, wouldn't anybody guess that you know something; and wouldn't they then want to know what you know and where you got it?"

"Not in this case. Because, as I said, Irene's daughter is already suspicious about how and where her mother died and has told me so. It doesn't make sense to her that her mom would be going to early mass, especially in that awful weather."

"So ... ?"

"So I'll be asking more than I'll be telling. Trust me. I won't give anything away or jeopardize even the possibility of that. Can you trust a ... veteran like me to pull that off?" he said, flashing a cajoling smile.

"Well ... maybe. But I'm still not a hundred percent sure."

"Think about it, please. I'm going to the restroom," Father John said, and rose awkwardly from his chair, his joints stiff from sitting.

When he returned, he asked: "Had enough time to think that over?"

"I guess so."

"Comfortable with my talking to Irene's family? Or comfortable enough, anyway?"

"I suppose. You will be careful, right?"

"You can be sure I will. I take confession and the seal of confession very seriously, Michael. Speaking of which – when can we get to your actual confession?"

"Now, I guess. I think you know most of what I want to say, Father."

"Just to be sure, can you quickly touch on those things again?"

"The major thing is the guilt I have about my Mom's death: moving her body, the stress I may have caused her ... you know." *He's still hedging his bets. Let it go, John.*

After adding several things of noticeably lesser magnitude, Michael finished with: "I'm heartily sorry for these and all the sins of my past life, promise to amend my life with the help of God's grace, and ask your forgiveness, Father, and God's."

Father John reassured him of the lack of complicity in his mother's death. He then assigned a noticeably light penance and gave him the forgiveness of absolution. Finally he asked Michael to join him in a moment of spontaneous prayer of gratitude for God's mercy.

And with that, it was over. Father John put his hand on Michael's shoulder and thanked him for his honesty and his trust in him. And Michael flashed a shy but grateful and relieved smile.

"Now – I still think we should stay in touch. I want to talk to Irene's family and then get back to you. I hope that will allow me to reassure you as to the legal ramifications of all this. I expect there'll be little or nothing for you to worry about, but I want to check and get back to you – and ease your mind on it all."

"Fine. Should I wait for you to call me, or do you want me to get hold of you some time tomorrow?"

"I'll call you. Will you be at home?"

"I should be, yes."

"What if you aren't? I can't say anything to your mother."

"Right. I have a cell phone. Let me give you that number."

He wrote it on a piece of paper that Father John tucked into his shirt pocket alongside his notebook. "But that brings up something we haven't touched on. Have you told your mother any of this?"

"No, I haven't."

"What are you planning to do about that?"

"I haven't figured that out yet."

"Why not think about it before you tell her anything, then talk to me first. As it sorts out in your mind, I'd be glad to be a sounding board for you. I'm of a mind that she should hear about all of it, but the timing has to be right. Anyway, it's your decision, okay?"

"I'll do that tonight."

"Good. Now, can you get me back to Hilary's?" he asked, smiling.

"Glad to," Michael said, and putting some money on the table for the waitress, he began to put on his jacket. "Thanks," he added, sincerely.

"You have no idea how glad I've been to do it, Michael," said Father John. And he meant every word of that.

When he'd been dropped off, he waved goodbye to Michael and watched him drive away. But he continued standing in the cold, dark night and reflected on something that just popped into his mind.

It was December twenty-first, the winter solstice and the longest night of the year. And with no moon, it was also the longest extremely dark night of the year. Father John couldn't help thinking of the Gospel of John, one that was special because he shared its name. It spoke of Jesus as light of the world and doing the deeds of light; and it warned against the night when things that were shameful could be done and hidden and no honest work could be done. Those texts seemed full of portent as he stood in the freezing darkness of that Chicago night.

He wondered how ancient peoples, or even those as recent as several hundred years ago, had felt when they were enveloped by such darkness. Were they afraid, he wondered. Probably. On moonless nights their world would have been a solidly black place where evil could thrive and all normal guarantees were forfeit and only the foolhardy would venture forth.

Perhaps that was why he liked Christmas so much: it was such a hope-filled feast. Early Christians had accepted the Roman celebration of the sun's annual return at this very time of year by christening – christianizing – that Roman feast of Sol Invictus, the unconquered sun. They re-named it Christmas and celebrated the birth of the Son of God, come with His light to redeem a world darkened by sin. It was such a nice pun in English: sun-son. But it didn't work in Latin.

Father John hoped that with the passing of the solstice that night, his modern world would be brought surely, if slowly, back into the light, and grace might grow and thrive, and deeds of darkness lose their power and presence, and God's light settle warmly over us all – just like the warm breast and bright wings of the Holy Ghost.

CHAPTER XII – NEIGHBORLINESS

After mass on Thursday, the twenty-second, there was a call for Father John.

"Hello?"

"Father Wintermann?"

"Yes ... "

"This is Nancy." When the priest hesitated slightly, she added: "Irene's daughter ... "

"Oh, yes. Pardon me. I guess I never got your name. Or at least it wasn't well imprinted in my memory. Sorry about that. I'm glad you're able to get back to me."

"No problem with that. But, sorry to say, I still have no report. I'd hoped to hear by now."

"I'm surprised that you haven't. While I imagine that not knowing is burdensome to you ..." *and to me too* " ... I suppose the best we can do is wait as patiently as possible. Unless ... do you have their number? You could call them."

"Yes, I do, and I'm going to do that if I don't hear before ten. But, you know, I just can't help thinking about that neighbor. I can't get him out of my head. Do you have a moment to talk about him? I mean, about the things he's done to make me so worried? Can I tell you of a couple of incidents involving the man?"

"Yes, that would be fine. But can you just give me the gist of them?"

"Yes, I can do that. First, there was that recent incident I already mentioned – last spring sometime – about the tree. But there was also a time when his dog messed over some of Mom's flowers. That was several years ago. When Mom mentioned it – nicely, she said, and I believe her – he was curt and not at all welcoming of the information ... and then did absolutely nothing about it.

"A few months later, his dog got loose again and threatened Mom in her own back yard. It was barking and showing its teeth, and it forced Mom onto her porch and back into the house. She was genuinely frightened. And when she phoned the man, he not only wouldn't come to remove the dog, but he was absolutely impolite about what he said and how he said it. Mom said she might have to call the police, and only then did he come for the dog. He has kept it firmly leashed since then, and there have been no recurrences. But the tree incident came on the heels of these things. Given the man's size and general unapproachability, I think my fears are reasonable. Wouldn't you agree?"

"Put that way, you have a point. You may well want to tell the police if the report doesn't rule out something untoward." Father John knew that talking to the police about the man wasn't really needed.

"I'm glad you agree with me about him. At a time like this it's hard to distinguish between normal, common-sense concerns and paranoia. Know what I mean?"

"I do. And I'm glad I could help reassure you. Hold off on the police and do call me as soon as you hear anything, won't you?"

"Thanks, Father. I'll call just as soon as I hear something. But before I hang up, would you mind talking to that neighbor? I know you think I shouldn't. But could you?"

It was a complication the priest wasn't happy about, but he couldn't think quickly enough how to refuse. "Do you really think that's necessary, or that it will help?" *Pretty lame, John – it's not going to do the trick.*

"Well, it might rule something out." She paused. "It would make me feel easier."

Trapped! "Okay, I'll do it as soon as I can. I don't know when the neighbor will be available. But I'll try." He was hoping against hope that the autopsy might have short-circuited this sort of thing by now. *Even so, there's still the issue of how and why Mrs. O'Carroll ended up outside church, and we're going to have to help Nancy get past that. Under the circumstances, who can blame her for worrying about that neighbor?*

"Oh, thank you. I'll call soon. Bye." And she was gone just that quickly.

I've been had! As he hung up, Father John said a quick prayer against further complications – further delays to his return to Algoma.

There was nothing to keep him from it, and he had promised, after all. So he donned his coat and, armed with Irene's address from the receptionist, set out to find the troublesome neighbor. He'd have to be living right next door to her.

Just as he arrived in front of the house on the near side of Mrs. O'Carroll's, he realized he might not encounter a living soul there, in which case his trip would be wasted and he'd be no closer to anything. But he'd come this far already and decided to take his chances. Surprisingly, the sidewalks were mostly cleared and he'd arrived in jig time.

The doorbell's first ring roused someone, a large man, and Father John could tell by even his first glimpse that this fellow was a little different. It had to be the right guy. He was as large as Nancy had intimated, his face was square and noncommittal, and his eyes were perhaps just a little too close together for Father John's taste. But the kicker was that he was dressed in an open-necked short-sleeved shirt. *In the middle of winter, for God's sake!*

Father John had his clerical collar on and made sure his coat was open just enough for it to be seen. He wanted all the leverage he could get. "Pardon me, but I'm Father John Wintermann. I'm staying for a few days at St. Hilary's because I came for Monday's funeral and got stranded by the ice storm."

The man continued staring at him. So Father John continued. "I've come about Mrs. O'Carroll next door."

"What about her?" The tone wasn't exactly gruff, but it was hardly friendly. The man had a deep voice.

"Are you aware that she's suffered a fall?"

"No. Are you collecting for her medical bills? If you are, I'm not interested." And he began to close the door.

"No," Father John said, sticking his hand out and holding the door open slightly. "I'm not collecting for anything. I've come to talk with you about her, if I may."

"So talk," the man said, leaving the door barely open and pointedly not inviting the priest inside.

The man's thick accent made him hard to understand, but Father John was undaunted and continued as politely as he could. "Actually, she died from that fall, and I'd very much like to talk to you about her. As her neighbor, I imagine you knew her at least a little bit."

"I didn't know her very good, and we don't get along good either," he said, honestly enough.

"So I understand. When did you see her last, and was she okay at that time?"

"I'm not talk to her in a lot of weeks. And I don't want to talk to you, either." He made another move to close the door.

But Father John persisted. "May I please come in?"

"I am busy. No. Please go away now." And this time he succeeded in getting the door closed. Angrily, it seemed to the priest.

There was nothing to do but retreat back down the steps and onto the sidewalk. He stood there a few moments, staring at the door and puzzling over his next move. Then he turned to retrace his steps to St. Hilary's.

He couldn't tell if the man was watching him from inside the house or not, but guessed that he wasn't. He had seemed less angry than disinterested, like he didn't want to be bothered or could care less about this stranger at his door. Whatever, it had been a highly unproductive moment, in Father John's estimation, except that he could now corroborate the negative image Nancy had given him. The man was not a very nice prospect to have next door, all right. And Father John felt like he had nothing to show for this exercise.

That was what he intended to convey to Nancy when they talked next, *which I hope is soon after I get back to Hilary's.*

No calls were awaiting him when he got back, so he decided to call Nancy. But he couldn't get her. He dutifully left a message, then wondered what to do with his time, because Michael hadn't called either. He went upstairs and began to pack. He was hoping against hope that he could get away the next morning.

When he came back downstairs, the receptionist heard his footsteps and called out: "Who's there?"

"Father Wintermann."

"Oh. There's a message for you. I didn't know where you were."

"I was in my room." By that time he had made it to her office door.

"Here," she said, handing him the piece of pink phone notepaper.

It was from Nancy. *Drat!* It stated simply that she felt she couldn't wait and had called the police about the neighbor. *Double drat! Why not talk to me first? And what about the autopsy? There's nothing here about the autopsy.*

He was getting uncharacteristically angry and took a moment to cool down. *Now what?* He stood in the doorway for a few moments, contemplating the piece of paper and thinking about his options, none of which seemed all that good, not to mention pleasant.

The staff person asked: "You all right, Father?"

"Yes. Oh, yes. I'm just puzzled about what to do about this note, is all. I'm fine. Thanks for asking."

"You're welcome," she said, and turned back to the work that had occupied her before he walked in.

I don't know where Bill is. Nancy's called the police on the neighbor. And I've got to protect what Michael's told me. Good grief! Nothing was coming to him, and Father John was almost at wit's end.

Did the police get there before or after me? After, I'd almost bet. The guy would've acted a whole lot different: angrier – or maybe just the opposite. Yeah, not angry. Scared or tamed – something like that. Maybe if I go back, he'll be more approachable. On that logic, he put on his coat and retraced his steps toward the man's house.

This time the gentleman did indeed act differently, but he still wasn't exactly friendly.

"You back again?"

"Yes. I'd really like to talk with you. May I?"

"You sent police here?"

"Police? No, I didn't send them," he said, with a quizzical look on his face. He hoped it looked innocent enough. After all, knowing they'd come was one thing. Sending them was something else entirely. And he could truthfully say he hadn't sent them. "May I please come in?"

The man debated a few seconds and then, without saying a word, reluctantly held the door open just wide enough for the priest to squeeze through, as though he were saving money on his heating bill.

"Thank you. I am Father John Wintermann, if you remember," he said, unbuttoning his coat but not taking it off.

Again the man said nothing, as if to say *get on with it, already*.

"Mrs. O'Carroll died from that fall, as I believe I've already told you. Her daughter knows that you and her mother had words a time or two. In her grief I think she wants to look into everything that might explain her mother's death, including the neighbor who didn't get along with her mom. Perhaps it was *she* who sent the police. As for myself, I don't want to believe that you had anything to do with her death … "

Until now the man's face looked icy, like he was backed into a corner and unable to do much about it. Now it changed to mild surprise.

Hadn't he understood that's why the police came?

Father John was continuing: "I'd like to reassure her daughter that's actually the case. So, you see, I have to talk to you. Thanks for letting me."

The man's countenance was softening with each passing second, but he was still silent.

So Father John kept talking. "When exactly did you talk with Mrs. O'Carroll last?"

"Like I say, many weeks now."

"So you didn't talk to her on Monday? Did you see her that day?"

"No."

"Did she have any visitors that you know of that day?"

"Monday I work. Did not see her or anyone."

"No one else came to her home on Monday?"

"I work. I saw no one."

Michael's visit and late-night departure were in all probability not known around the neighborhood, Father John now realized. *No one else has come forward, and this man, the closest neighbor and the most likely to see something, hadn't seen a thing. What a relief!*

"Let me just reassure you that an argument or two doesn't prove you had anything to do with her death, Mister … ah … I'm sorry, but what is your name?"

"Kwiatkowski." He gave it the Polish pronunciation, changing each "w" to a "v".

"Mr. Kwiatkowski – thank you. That doesn't prove anything at all, as I said. But I hope you can see why Irene's daughter would have been concerned and would naturally have thought of you. I promise you that I will reassure her she needn't concern herself about that any more. And I hope that you don't have any more problems with the police, Mr. Kwiatkowski. But if you should happen to, please call St. Hilary's immediately. You know where that is, just down the street, right?"

"Yes, I know. I go there."

"And you have their number, or you can find it, can't you?"

"Yes."

"Good." He realized there would probably never be such a call to the rectory, but if there were, he hoped Bill would forgive him for suggesting that.

"Well, I suppose I'll be getting back now. Thanks again for your time." He turned to let himself out. His last look at Mr. Kwiatkowski showed a picture of stunned surprise, like the man hardly knew what had hit him. But the large, stolid – and largely monosyllabic – man didn't look displeased. That was something, anyway.

CHAPTER XIII – AUTOPSY

Bill was at a nearby hospital but was expected back momentarily. With just coffee for his breakfast, something to eat suddenly sounded like a very nice thing to Father John. He spoke to the receptionist and was told that when the staff was present, they usually shared something brought in for lunch, and Father Bill was probably picking that up as they spoke.

"Good! I'll run to my room and tidy up. Let me know when he returns."

"Will do, Father."

He headed upstairs, where he made his bed – it had certainly aired enough by then – and used the facilities. He had barely stepped out of the bathroom when the intercom buzzed to summon him to the kitchen.

"Hello." Father John said, drawing out the word as he entered the kitchen from the back stairs. "Am I glad to see you, Bill. I could eat a horse."

"You'll be happy to know that's what I have here: a horse meat sandwich, just for you. The rest of us are having Italian beef," Bill said, grinning. And they all sat down at the kitchen table to do justice to the subs that Bill was spreading around the table.

The camaraderie and banter was delightful to Father John, who spent the first few minutes silently eyeing the others as he ate his sandwich – ham, as it turned out, for Bill had actually brought a variety of choices. He watched the goings on with no little jealousy.

You miss out on that when you're the only guy in a small-town rectory without a parish staff. They sure enjoy one another.

"Staying tonight again, John?" Bill asked.

"Looks like it. Heard anything about the roads?"

"The streets are negotiable – just fine, in fact. I know the expressways are too, but I don't know about the interstates outside the metro area. Though, my guess is that they're okay too."

"Well, much as I hate to delay, I want to see this O'Carroll thing through. I'm hoping I can leave tomorrow. I hate to call the state police to ask about roads because every time I do that down south I just get dire messages as to how unsafe it is to travel. And that's not always the case in actuality. I think they just err on the side of caution all the time, to protect travelers or maybe to keep their own workload down."

Bill laughed, and so did two of the ladies who were eating with them. "Same thing here."

"You know," Father John said, "I could kill two birds with one stone and check in with my parish." He realized he hadn't gotten to them yet that day. *So much for making mental notes!* "They may know something about the roads between there and here. I don't imagine they have any problems down south, but maybe there are some statewide bulletins they've picked up on. There may even be information at the town truck stop. Truckers are good for that kind of information. Think I'll do that when we're finished eating."

It took twenty minutes of joking, eating and cleaning up before he got time to make that call. He talked more than twenty minutes because he had instructions for various people about the

Christmas services as well as the news that he probably couldn't travel yet. Then he had to hear about the continuing obstacles the parish committee was encountering readying Annie's mansion for public viewing. *They've only been at it how long now? Three months – or more! Ever since we inherited it in September. Patience, John!*

The bad news was, the committee thought it would take 'til spring. The good news was that Horace Denver was giving them another painting or two from the upstairs studio. He told them to be sure to phrase it just that way for Father John: the upstairs studio.

The secretary asked what that meant, and he had to explain that Annie kept one room upstairs rather secluded, not even letting Maisie clean there. It was in effect her studio where she painted over the years. Or, perhaps, it was simply where she stored her canvases, because, Father John explained, it was unbearably hot up there in the summer, and he couldn't imagine anyone being able to work on that floor. Besides, there was little natural light in that particular room. *Horace probably wants me to know that those paintings have never been seen before.*

After asking how everyone was and learning that everything was fine in town and parish, he hung up. He was glad to know there were no crises. *Goodness knows I have enough here!* But he didn't know what to make of the fact that there seemed little anxiety about his still being stuck up north. *Maybe I'm not as important to St. Helena's as I think.* As for the roads, all they knew was that things were fine down their way. It was cool but clear, and no precipitation. "Hasn't been any since you left, Father."

With still no word from Nancy, he decided to kill some more time and call Fred and Frieda Becker. He hadn't talked to them in over a week, and maybe they had some news worth sharing. "Hi. Father John here. Got a minute?"

He had reached Frieda, who whooped gleefully when she realized who it was and shouted the news to her husband in the back of the drugstore. "I'm fine. Where are you? And why are you callin' on the phone? Come on over for coffee."

"Oh, I'm still in Chicago. Had an ice storm here Tuesday morning and I'm still stranded. You hear about that piece of nasty weather?"

"Dunno – who pays attention to Chicago weather? You're okay, otherwise? Just stranded?"

"Yes, that's about it. I was wondering if you'd heard anything from around town."

"Not much. Mostly the usual stuff, you know: births, deaths, the usual. Oh, yeah – the mayor's daughter had a baby down in Royalton. Did you know her?"

He hadn't but told her to send regards to the mayor for him. "And explain why I can't do that myself just now, while you're at it. Anything else?"

"Herb over at the Smile nearly got pneumonia, working out on his son-in-law's farm the other day. Stayed out too long in the cold and got wet down by the pond. Came in for some cold medicine, but Fred thought he was just plain lucky it wasn't anything worse. Damn fool, if you ask me. Shouldn't be out in the cold and wet like that, 'specially at his age." But she chuckled as she said it.

"I was wondering if you'd ever heard anything else about Wesley Young. I know he moved away, but do you know where, or how he's doing?"

"Not a thing. The man's dropped off the face of the earth. His home finally sold on Monday, matter of fact. Suppose you could ask Butterworth Realty, if you really needed to know."

"Thanks. I'll keep that in mind." But he didn't intend to do that. Asking Fred and Frieda was okay, but he didn't want to involve some realtor in his curiosity. That could easily get back to Mr. Young, who might not take it kindly that the priest was checking after him.

"Well, I was just missing you and thought I'd give you a buzz. Nice talking to you, Frieda. Tell Fred hello. I'll be home in a day or so. Can't miss the Christmas services, you know. Even if I have to drive through ice – and I don't want to – I'll be there." And he hung up.

When he got off the phone, the receptionist must have noticed that the light that indicated his phone had gone out. She buzzed. "Nancy just called. You can probably reach her at her home if you're quick. She said she'd be leaving shortly."

He was able to get her and said first off how glad he was at not having to play more phone tag. He was about to mention Mr. Kwiatkowski when she said she had the autopsy results.

"Great. What did you learn?"

"They called just after we talked earlier, and I forgot to give that to you when I left my message. Sorry. You were right about it maybe being something natural. Mom had a stroke. But," and she drew out the rest of her sentence for dramatic effect, "she didn't die from that. The report said it was a blow to her head that was the cause of death."

Father John's mind was racing. *The way she sounds, that doesn't satisfy her.* "What does that tell you, Nancy?" Father John was stalling for time by throwing the ball into her court.

"She could have fallen as a result of the stroke, I suppose, Father."

Bingo!

"But I still don't think she would have gone to early mass like that. Do you? I think you said that didn't make any sense to you either, right?"

The logic's perfect – now what do I do? "Yes I did say that, and it does boggle the mind. Father Bill told me that while it wasn't completely out of the question for your mom to come to mass during the week, it wasn't really like her. So the real issue is that awful weather plus how early she'd have had to start out for me to find her so much before mass like I did. But let's keep thinking about this. Perhaps if we brainstorm a bit, we'll hit on something." *Keep talking, John – you've got to come up with something.* "Can you come over? We could put both our minds to it."

"If you think it might help ... "

"Can't hurt. Got the time to come now?"

"I could."

"Fine. I'll see you in a few minutes. That is, I imagine you can make it here that soon. Pardon me, but I don't know where you live, so maybe I'm presuming too much here."

"I can be there shortly, Father, but I have an errand to run first. I was almost out of the house with that when you called."

"So when should I expect you?"

"Less than an hour. That should work."

"Good. You know where I am, right?"

"Hilary's. Bryn Mawr and California."

"Yes. And you can park either on Bryn Mawr or on the side street alongside the rectory. That's Fairfield. But it's one-way, and to make it work you'll have to go a couple of blocks north of Bryn Mawr on Lincoln to catch Fairfield on your left."

"Thanks for the tip. See you soon."

When he put the phone down, he realized he hadn't told her about Mr. Kwiatkowski. *Must remember to do that when she gets here. More importantly, I'd better figure out some angles we can explore. God, this is getting tricky!*

After he'd ordered his thoughts, he went into the receptionist's office to chat while waiting for Nancy. She arrived thirty minutes after the phone conversation – earlier than he'd expected.

"Thanks for coming. We can talk in here, I believe," he said, leading her into the small office he'd been using a lot lately.

"I'm glad we can get together, Father, because this death of my mother's seems to be getting curiouser and curiouser." She looked better than he had pictured her, taller and quite attractive.

"Oh," was all the priest could say as he wondered what further knots things could possibly be twisted into.

"Yes. Coming over here I stopped past Mom's safety deposit box to get her will. It's very interesting. I wonder if she had some sort of premonition."

"Why would you say that, Nancy?"

"Oh, I don't know. We decided to redo her will when Dad died, but she didn't get to it immediately. It was finally done about a year ago. She leaves predictable things to predictable people, all right – I'll inherit the house and most of its contents – no surprise there. Mementos are marked for various relatives and friends – all of these were more or less foregone conclusions too. But then she makes a point of leaving something to her son."

"Your brother – he died, didn't he?" asked Father John, not giving other possibilities a thought.

"Yes. And that's what's so strange."

"How so? You think your mother had gone senile and forgotten that?"

"No, I doubt that. But, given my confidence in her sound mind, consider how recently this will was drawn up."

"So," he said, drawing out the word before continuing: "what do you think it means?" He still hadn't thought about Michael.

"I don't know. It's troubling. There was nothing in any earlier draft about her son – not since he died years ago. But in this one, she makes this addition, and she also said that there's an envelope clearly marked for him spelling out his bequest. But," she said slowly for effect: "there's no such envelope in the deposit box and it's not indicated in the will where it should be found."

"Maybe she merely forgot to mention that detail. You'll come across it when you sort through her effects, don't you think? And then you can make sense of it. Your brother's death won't be hard to verify for the court, I'm sure." He had yet to put the obvious together in his mind, and the puzzled look on his face was genuine.

"That's not like Mom at all, Father. She was neat as a pin, thorough and well-prepared for everything she ever did." Father John thought of Michael's mention of *scrubby-Dutch* and smiled. But then it hit him: *Michael! Irene didn't know his name at the time she did the will, so she didn't use a name. She must have put that into the will just in case he turned up. And that means he was still very much on her mind. Good Lord!*

Nancy noticed the beginnings of a smile on his face, and asked about it.

Father John thought fast. "Oh, I'm just remembering some similar surprises in a will last September. An old lady in my parish died and she surprised all kinds of people with what she left and to whom she left it. Sorry to have gotten so lost in my own thoughts like that." *Thank God for Annie! But now I also have to get that image of the old lady on the can of Old Dutch Cleanser out of my mind.* And he almost grinned again.

"So then," he continued, "what's to be done about that? Start ransacking the house? I mean, it's not going to make much sense 'til you find that envelope, will it?"

"I suppose not, but it's surely strange. Another strange thing."

"Perhaps in the meantime I could tell you that I saw her neighbor, Mr. Kwiatkowski." He pronounced the name the same way he'd heard it. "I was surprised you called the police. I thought you were going to wait 'til we heard about the autopsy."

"I did wait. I called after I got the results. It still doesn't make sense that she was at church," she said emphatically.

"Oh. Since you hadn't left any message for me about the results, I assumed you didn't have them yet."

"Sorry about that. I guess I'm pretty rattled these days. Should have told you."

"Well, it may have been a blessing in disguise, as it turned out. I saw him before you called the police, or at least before they'd gotten to him. He was pretty unapproachable, to put it nicely. When I went back, which I did the moment I heard you'd told the cops, he even let me in – and we had what I would call a satisfactory chat. And before I forget to ask, why did you have them see him? I mean, did you place him under suspicion for her death, or what?"

"No, I just mentioned the uncomfortable incidents. I'm not sure the desk sergeant with whom I talked even knew of Mom's death. He hung up pretty quick – he might have had several things happening at once there. Anyway, he promised someone would stop past. For all I knew, he may have only received a warning to chill out."

"Well, having the long arm of the law show up at his door must have put the fear of the Lord in Mr. Kwiatkowski, though – he was pretty forthcoming that second time. Poor guy, he must be shook up … or confused. At very least the cops didn't help his paranoia any. He told me that he hadn't seen or talked to your mom in a while. And I believe him. I really don't think he did anything to your mother."

"If you say so. But I'm not willing to forget about him just yet. Mom's being found on a cold church step still doesn't sit well with me. Something's goofy there. And that guy's big enough he could have done something to her and then moved her body."

"Well, we can't do much more than file that in the back of our heads right now, can we? Not until we come up with something here. Remember? Brainstorming!"

"Right. Got any ideas? I didn't come up with any."

"Well, for one thing, let me ask if the autopsy report spoke of any bruises on your mother?"

"I don't recall. Why's that important?"

"If she'd been knocked down, forcibly caused to fall, there should be bruises where she was manhandled. No?"

"That makes sense. But we already know the cause of death was the blow to her head, remember. And she could've been caused to fall."

"But no bruises plus the stroke, Nancy – that doesn't indicate some forcible attempt on her life to me. Think about it. Can you agree with me on that?"

"Well, you may have a point. But what about the church steps?"

"Well, let's go at this methodically. We've just ruled out murder, manslaughter and the like – correct?"

"Yes," she said, her voice rising slightly at she finished the word, indicating her lack of understanding as to where this was heading.

"So the continued concern about your mother dying outside church is … ?"

"It's still weird – makes no sense," she said.

"But you don't connect it in any way with murder, etc.?"

"Correct. But… Maybe Mom was exhibiting some erratic behavior," she said, enlightened with an unpleasant possibility. "I mean, if that thing in the will's peculiar, maybe she was doing some other strange things. And might that not be a precursor to a stroke?" She didn't like the roll she was on.

"Hold on," Father John said. "I know we're brainstorming, but let me comment. I don't know much about strokes, but that part doesn't seem accurate."

"What part?"

"About erratic behavior being an indicator or a precursor of a stroke. I don't think you can link those things like that."

"Okay, but what about the possibility of a string of odd things, connected to a stroke or not?"

"Maybe," Father John conceded, "but do you really have evidence of any other such things?" He was hoping for a way out of this tangle, but not through something so completely out of character like that. From what Michael had said, he couldn't see how any of this fit Irene.

"No, I don't – there's nothing else I'm aware of, really," she said haltingly.

"Well, maybe we can rule that out too, then. No erratic stuff."

"But we're still left with her being found outside church. And that bothers me. And the son thing in the will, too."

The secretary knocked on the door. "Yes," Father John said.

"Call for you, Father. From Algoma."

"Sorry," Father John started to apologize, but Nancy cut him short.

"It's okay, Father. I don't think we're getting anywhere here, and I've tons of things hanging over me with funeral arrangements."

"I understand. You'll be wanting to get on your way." He couldn't say he was sorry for her early departure. "But, let me ask: have you set a time for the funeral?"

"Yes. We've – I've – decided on Saturday afternoon. Haven't set the time in stone yet, but probably shortly after noon. The office here can tell you when we settle it with the funeral home and Father Bill."

Father John's eyebrows shot up. "Saturday afternoon?"

"Father Bill wasn't wild about it but said he'd do it. It will have to be before confessions and evening mass. But it's not official yet."

"Well, stay in touch. We'll unravel this yet, I promise." But while his face and voice showed hope, he didn't feel that hopeful.

He saw her out, and when he'd closed the front door behind her, he went to get his phone call.

CHAPTER XIV – COMPLICATIONS

It was Algoma again.

"Father, something terrible has happened. Johnny Werther had a stroke and is at St. Luke's."

"When?"

"Just an hour ago or so. They've been trying to reach you and finally called me. I don't know why they didn't call Shirley at home." Shirley Detmer, the parish secretary, generally came to work only once or twice a week. This was Jane Giraldo, St. Helena's organist.

"Did you tell them I was stuck up here because of the ice?"

"I didn't know anything about that, sorry – only found it out from Shirley when I called her at home just now. I figured she'd know where you were. Rather than make her call you, though, I decided to, since I knew the most about Johnny's condition."

"I appreciate your taking that trouble, Jane. Have you told the hospital to get another priest to anoint him? Someone's surely on call."

"Yes, I did, and they told me they'd get someone."

"Good. So, is that the latest about Johnny, then? Do you know anything further?"

"Not good, Father. The stroke was massive. They're not even sure he'll survive. But the ER nurse told me that if he did, she was afraid he might be a vegetable. Isn't that awful!" She was near tears.

Johnny was a stalwart member of the parish and had been active for as long as anyone could remember in all the physical stuff parishes need every so often. If there were chairs to move, he was there; in the years when they used to have the parish festival, Johnny would work the set-up and the take-down, and often volunteered in a booth or two during the festival itself, as well. Retired from government work a few years now, he was even more available but wasn't really that old, for all that, perhaps his mid-sixties: not much older than himself, Father John knew. He had a deep affection for the pudgy, jolly, faithful worker, and he felt very bad he couldn't be at his bedside, even though Johnny might not recognize him or anyone, given his condition. His infectious smile and tireless willingness to do anything for the parish had been for years an inspiration to more than just his pastor.

"Jane, I don't blame you for being upset. I am. It's so sad that such an active and generous man should be brought so low – and so suddenly. Can you start the prayer chain by calling your people on the list? I'm sorry to have to say that getting home in time for a funeral, if there is to be one, is up in the air. I hold out hope of getting on the road soon – maybe tomorrow, but it's still not good up here."

"I'm on it, Father. Fact is, I plan to do my part of the chain just after I reached you. Shirley's got the rest of it going by now, I'm sure. She said she'd be at it as soon as we hung up on each other. Johnny's almost certainly not gotten a room yet, Father. But I'll bet you can reach his family in the emergency room."

"I'll do that. And thanks again, Jane."

He hung up feeling sad on top of the curious mixture of stressful feelings that St. Hilary's had been laying on his shoulders. He picked up the phone immediately to call Burger. He knew the hospital number by heart.

In no time he was talking to Johnny's wife, who seemed to be holding up surprisingly well, under the circumstances. She was with one of her sons. The other son and her only daughter lived in the St. Louis suburbs, and they'd already been told. She thought they were probably on their way by now. "I'm okay, Father. I'm praying he'll come out of this. People do all the time, you know."

"Yes, they do, Fay. And I'll be praying right along with you. I'm told that one of the other priests will be in, if that hasn't happened already, to anoint Johnny. Do you know if he's arrived yet?"

"Not that I know of, Father ... "

"Well, make sure the charge nurse knows you want to be with your husband when he does get there. Depending on what the medical folks are doing at the time, they may not allow many people in with the priest, but there'll be room for you. And be sure to ask for anyone else who wants to join you. The most they can do is say no."

She laughed gently. "I won't be bashful, Father. I couldn't live with myself if I weren't with Johnny as much as possible."

"Go for it, gal," Father said. His light-hearted remark once again drew a quiet giggle.

"You know I will, Father."

"Jane and Shirley both know how to get me if you need me again. I'm stuck in Chicago after Mrs. Restorski's funeral because of a freak ice storm. But you can count on my prayers – don't ever question it. I'll not keep you longer – I know you may get a chance to be with Johnny any moment now."

"Bye, Father. Thanks for calling."

He silently shook his head as he put the phone in its cradle and offered the first of his promised prayers. *Of all the rotten luck – and at Christmas too! Isn't that the way it goes? Holidays! Massive stroke – and a vegetable maybe. How awful!*

Wait a minute – massive *stroke? I wonder if Irene's stroke was massive. Nancy didn't say. If it was, perhaps that might have been* her *prognosis if she hadn't died from cracking her skull like that. And then, maybe Nancy will think differently about wanting to pursue the business of her being found outside church. I'll ask her to review the exact wording of that report as soon as I get the chance to talk to her again.*

But he knew that before anything else, he wanted to talk to Michael. *He needs to hear about that postmortem.*

Father John went right back to the phone after fishing Michael's number out of his shirt pocket. Moments later he had him on the line.

"Michael, Father John. I just heard from Irene's daughter. The autopsy indicated that Irene had a stroke. They also concluded that it was the fall that killed her."

"She didn't trip, then? It was a ... ?"

"A stroke – that's right. I don't know what triggered it, and I doubt that they do. We'll probably never know. At times like this, people tend to say things like 'it was her time.' Who knows? But so far as your involvement goes, it was a natural occurrence and you plainly had no control over that."

"Yes," he said hesitantly.

"Are you able to talk freely, Michael?" He sensed caution in Michael's terse answers.

"Not really."

"Can you get to a public phone, so we can continue this?"

"Give me some time on that."

"Okay. Should I wait here for your call?"

"Yes."

"What do you think? You can call in fifteen minutes, maybe?"

"I think so."

"When you do, be sure to tell me if it's going to cost you a bunch of change to make the call, because I can call you back."

"I will, but it shouldn't."

"Shouldn't cost extra, you mean."

"Right."

"Well, then, I'll be waiting."

"Goodbye."

It took twenty minutes, and Father John got on the line immediately. "You okay?"

"Yeah, I think so."

"The reason I wanted to keep talking is to explore the implications of the seal of confession further with you. There are options now, and you need to think them through."

"Like what, Father?"

"Well, you may want me to tell Irene's daughter, Nancy, some of what we've talked about, all of it or none of it. And each choice has certain consequences, you see."

"Keep talking, Father."

"Nancy is suspicious about her mother ending up outside church. She knows that the report shows her mother died of natural causes, that she wasn't killed, that is – no murder, no crime. But it still makes little sense to her that Irene was found at church. She doesn't know what to make of that, and it bothers her. It wasn't like her mom to go to daily mass, especially the early one, and most especially in such bad weather.

"So … you may want me to reason with her about having heard a confession, etc. etc. That is, I'd tell her only that the person who confessed to me panicked and moved the body. That's scenario number one. We'd hope that it would be enough to satisfy her and the matter could end there.

"Number two involves my finding out if she wants to meet the person who confessed to me. If you choose that one, you would have to decide just how much you want to say about Irene having given birth to you. Or maybe you decide you want that revealed, but you ask me to do the revealing. In either case, we hope it ends with that.

"Number three involves telling her everything from the git go, either through me, or in a conversation between the two of you, or maybe even one involving me."

He paused for breath, and when Michael didn't break in with a comment or question, he continued. "Now, I imagine you might want, or probably need, to think about all this, because with any of these possibilities, it's impossible to know exactly where things will go once the conversation begins. So you need to think about how to handle things no matter how she reacts – and there are a lot of possible reactions she could choose.

"If you need time, give me a call when you're ready. It could be even later tonight – or else early tomorrow, but, do it as soon as you can, please. I'm sorry to hurry you, but a number of things suggest that we shouldn't dawdle, among them the fact that Irene's funeral is being planned as we speak, and Nancy won't have much time to spare. We'll have to get our foot in her door, so to speak. So get back to me pronto."

"I realize what you're saying. And, I think, Father, that I do want some time to think about all that you've said. This is complicated, after all."

"No problem. When do you think you might be ready to talk again?"

"I'll try to call you this evening, before it gets too late. Will you be around?"

"I'll make it my business to be, Michael. And I'll be glad to help you work your way through this further when you do call."

"Good. Until tonight, then." And he hung up.

Father John speculated what the young man would do. He was guessing he would want to tell Nancy only the bare minimum. And he was determined that he would not pressure the lad – one way or the other.

But right now, it would be nice if I can get back to Nancy about what kind of stroke Irene had. It may affect what Michael does or doesn't need to say to her. Not sure I can reach her, though. Think she's had enough time to get back home yet? What the heck, she's got a machine – I'll call.

He got her machine. "Hello, Nancy. I realize that we just spoke, but something occurred to me about that report. Can you call me back as soon as possible? And please have the report nearby so we can check something in it."

Now he'd have to wait. There were lots of things and people to pray for. *Not a bad way to spend the time.*

CHAPTER XV – CONFIDENTIALITY

But as he left the room, he saw Bill in the other office. "Got a moment?" he asked.

"Sure. What's up?"

"I'd like to chat about a couple of things. Perhaps we could go upstairs to your room?"

"Fine. Go on up, I've got to finish something here with Mary Lou," and he turned back to the lady behind the desk.

Father John settled down into one of the comfortable chairs in Bill's nicely appointed apartment and waited. It didn't take long before Bill appeared and announced that it might be time for a drink soon.

"Never a bad idea, but I can wait a few minutes, 'til I get this off my chest, anyway."

"Fine, Bill said, "but don't make it too long – I've hankering fer a bourbon and branch," he said with a deliberately horrible Texas twang and a wink. He sat down on the couch and said: "Shoot."

"That another pun?" When Bill looked quizzical, Father John explained: "Texas twang, shoot!"

"Oh. No, not intended."

"Kind of lame, anyway. To the point: I'm sitting on top of some confidential stuff, and if I remember my moral theology, I can bring that – or some of it, anyway – to one other prudent person, can't I?"

"Depends."

"On what? You're already guessing the one prudent person is yourself, right?"

"Yes, but that's not what it depends on."

"So … ?" Father John said, encouraging him to keep going.

"It depends on whether I might be involved with whatever it is you want to run past me. And, since I'm the pastor here, I suspect I might well be involved – at very least peripherally."

"Well, yes. I suppose you're right about that."

"Then, as I remember my moral theology – or maybe it's just my common sense – perhaps you should just keep that to yourself."

"I'm afraid you might be right, now that I think about it. So that's what I'll just have to do. And in that case, what about that drink you were speaking of?"

"Fine," Bill said as he rose from the couch. "Follow me." He headed out the door and down the corridor to the common room. They were soon nursing a straight scotch and a bourbon and water, respectively, ice cubes gently clinking in their glasses the only sound in the otherwise quiet room.

After staring into his drink for a moment, Father John finally spoke. He figured Bill had been waiting to allow him the first words, anyway. "Heard anything about the roads?"

"No, not the outlying highways you're interested in. But I can't imagine that they wouldn't be thoroughly passable by now."

"Good. At least I know that I can probably get away whenever I choose now. My folks down south thought that too. But I'll still be hanging around at least 'til tomorrow sometime. If I have to wait 'til Christmas Eve, that will be bad."

"What's holding you up? Mrs. O'Carroll's death?"

"Yeah."

"And that's what's troubling you? What you wanted to speak about?"

"Some of it, yes. But, you know, I can still talk about part of it without breaching confidentiality. Her neighbor, for instance – you said you didn't really know much about him, but you were on target about his being different – difficult, as well. And that's pretty much what her daughter said, too. Did you know that he and Mrs. O'Carroll had a tiff or two – initiated, I might add, by Mr. Kwiatkowski?"

"Oh," was all Father Bill said, indicating that it was news to him and encouraging him to elaborate.

"Yes. He groused with her about a tree that was dropping limbs into his yard. And when his dog got loose and threatened Mrs. O'Carroll, he didn't really do anything about it at the time. Since then, Nancy has allowed, he has kept his dog locked up and apparently has done so up to the present. But, you know, when I first talked to him, he was not Mister Nice Guy, by a long shot."

"The first time?"

"Yeah. I went back after I learned that Nancy sent the police over to see him."

"She did?" He asked, his eyebrows up. "What for? Did she think he'd committed some sort of crime with that dog thing?"

"No, not that – she's upset that her mom was found here at church, and it doesn't make sense to her. She was toying with the idea that this aggressive guy might have done something to her mom. It's complicated, but she called the police after learning from the autopsy that her mother had a stroke and then died from severely bumping her head."

"Didn't know that," Bill interjected quickly.

"Yeah," John continued, "but she said she must have caught the desk sergeant at a busy time because she didn't get to fully explain herself before he promised to send someone over there and then hung up on her. So I'm not sure what exactly the cops discussed with the man, but they were surely there – probably just after I'd talked with him – and by the time I got back, all I know is that he was a whole lot more approachable."

"You think he did something?"

"I suppose if you stretch it a bit, he's capable. So it doesn't surprise me that he popped into Nancy's mind at a time like this. But as to his actually doing something … I don't think so. I just think he's a loner who's also a bit overwhelmed in a foreign culture, and his social skills lack, shall we say, fine-tuning."

Father Bill smiled. "Nicely put. So if he's out of the picture, where does that leave Nancy?"

"That's the sixty-four-thousand dollar question. I'm hoping she'll get back to me. I hate to see her upset about what to her are loose ends to her mom's death. But I would also like to get home, you know."

"I can imagine. I'm on top of the upcoming festivities here. But then, I've got a staff – and a good one. You don't have that luxury, do you?"

"Yes, and no. No staff, all right. But volunteers are on top of things this year, as they've always been. It's not the overall picture I'm worried about. It's more my piece of it. To tell the truth, it's more of an inconvenience. But, if you understand what I mean, it's *my* inconvenience," He smiled at the self-deprecating statement … smiled at himself, really. "And I've absolutely got to be back for Christmas Eve!"

Bill smiled, too. "Think I understand. But is that all that's got your shorts in a knot?"

"No. There's more. But I think your words were on target. I can keep the rest to myself. It will work out. You gotta believe, right?" he said, and smiled again.

"Yeah. Sometimes easier said than done, though. But … " Whatever he might have intended to say, he apparently changed his mind and looked down at his glass. "Not bad, eh? Especially this time of day," he said, holding his glass up. "Interested in some supper?" And when Father John didn't immediately respond, he added: "Eventually?"

"Yes, I am, but I'd like to wait a little for a phone call, if you don't mind. I'm hoping Nancy will get back to me." *And Michael.* Although that went unsaid.

"We can wait. But, you know, a message can be taken."

"You do have a point. Tell you what. If there's no call by the time we finish our drinks, we can go. What do you have in mind?"

"What about Italian?"

"Sounds good to me. Will you let me pay tonight?"

"Maybe. But if you're going to do that, I need to pick a more expensive place than the one I had been thinking of," he said, grinning.

Ten minutes later they were on their way to supper. And a nice meal it was, John had to admit. Even if he didn't get to do anything but leave the tip.

CHAPTER XVI – MICHAEL

When the two priests returned, there was a message for Father John. But it wasn't from Nancy. Michael had called. *Actually, that might be the better order in which to talk to them: Michael, then Nancy.*

"Hello?" Michael's voice said hesitantly.

"It's Father John, Michael."

"I hoped it might be. Thanks for calling back. Want to talk?"

"Yes. Can you come up?"

"Yes. I'm on my way."

Father John used the next fifty minutes to pray for Johnny Werther and the growing number of sick and deceased people he'd been steadily inheriting over the past few days.

When the two were finally together, Father John began: "Are you okay?"

"Yes. And I think I know some of what I want to do."

"Good, but let me just tell you first that I haven't been able to talk with Irene's family yet. I've left a message but haven't heard a thing. Maybe I will before we're finished. Okay, now, what is it that you've decided?"

"About Mom, first. I think I should tell her everything. Well, almost everything. She knows that I saw Mrs. O'Carroll, of course, and she thinks I've been coming up here to keep talking to her. So far I've told her that Mrs. O'Carroll is very interesting and she's full of stories about her husband but that she's been slow getting around to telling me all about Dad. What I'm not sure about is how to tell her Mrs. O'Carroll has died."

"Why not tell her all about your dad's war record. You may even want to show her Pat's letter, the one he never got around to sending. And, for the meantime, leave it at that. I think you should eventually tell her everything, including about the adoption, and of course about her death. But I also think you want to settle things with Irene's family first. I just think that's better timing. Does that make any sense?"

"I think it does, yes. And that's what I'll do tonight, if it's not too late when I get back. Or else tomorrow."

"Okay. Now, what about Irene's family?"

"That's more complicated. It almost looks to me like I should tell them everything, but I'm afraid I may go to jail, Father."

"I really don't think that will happen, Michael. But I grant you shouldn't be cavalier about it. I suppose if I were in your shoes, I might be afraid too."

"Well, because of that, I'd like to explore the possibility of just telling a little bit."

"Like what?"

"That's what I get hung up on – I'm not exactly sure how much to say. I believe I should let them know about being Irene's son. But I think if I did that, her family might think less of her. That would be awful to ruin someone's reputation like that, especially at the end of her life. So I'm torn about that."

"There are no perfect choices, Michael … "

Michael cut in: "Right. It just seems that whatever I say, someone will get hurt: me, or them, or both."

"Well, as I was going to say," Father John continued, "there may be some good possibilities nonetheless – not perfect, but good."

"Like what? I can't see any, Father – nothing clear-cut, for sure."

"Well, let's start with what's troubling her family. Irene's daughter can't get over her mom dying outside church. What about telling her the truth? You were with her mother when she had her stroke and you panicked. Moving the body to the church entrance just seemed like the best way to avoid embarrassment. After all, you didn't kill Irene. And since she was Catholic, going to mass was believable – and dying outside church was plausible. That is what you were thinking, correct?"

"Yes."

"So why not tell her daughter that?"

"If I were that daughter, I think I'd call the police if someone told me that."

"That's where I come in. I already told you that I believe I can initiate that discussion with her daughter – whose name is Nancy, by the way – and not even need to bring up your name. Seal of confession, you know."

"I don't know, Father. I'm not comfortable with that."

"Well, then, what else do you propose?"

"I don't know – I'm in a muddle, frankly. If only that ice hadn't happened!"

"Well, you're right about that. That ice complicated a whole lot of things for a whole lot of people. But … "

"I know." Michael broke in again: "Spilt milk!"

"Right. What are you of a mind to do, then?"

"I told you: I don't know. I've run myself in circles and that's why I wanted to talk to you. I was hoping you'd see something clearer than I can in this mess. Can you maybe go over those things you mentioned when we last talked?"

"They weren't real proposals, Michael, they were just an outline of the possibilities. I said you might want to tell some, all or nothing of this to Irene's family – and that you should go home and think about it. It seems to me that now you don't want to say anything. Or, maybe more accurately, you don't know what to say and therefore may be reduced to saying nothing."

"Yeah. Do you think I can do that? Will saying nothing work?"

"Michael, I'm not sure what will 'work' here. I can't accurately predict how people with free will may react to anything you may or may not do. But I suspect you need to say *something*. I'll try to walk you through some probabilities."

"Please, Father, do that."

"All right, as long as you understand a few qualifications. You and I are speculating, first of all. Second, we're not speculating about morality so much as about legalities or peripherally legal things. And, most of all, we're speculating about how these things will be accepted by Irene's family – by her daughter, really. So far, so good?"

"I think so. Keep talking, and if you lose me, we can back up and go over it again, right?"

"Right. Well then, the big issue with Irene's daughter is the mass thing – Irene almost never went to weekday mass. You couldn't know that, of course, but Nancy did, and even Father Bill confirmed it. And worse, she almost certainly wouldn't have gone in that ice. So … that's the sticking point with Nancy, and that's what we've got to deal with to satisfy her. Okay so far?"

"So far, yes."

"How to do that? I think you either don't say a word, and they don't find out you were at her home, or you tell Nancy what I said a moment ago, that you panicked."

"But won't I have to tell her about my being her son?"

"Maybe, maybe not. Depends. Do you want to do that?"

"Not if it ruins Irene's reputation."

"Does it have to?"

"I can't imagine that it wouldn't. I mean, you'd think less of someone who had an illegitimate child, wouldn't you?"

"Michael, you may be asking the wrong person. That's the last thing that crosses my mind when I'm confronted with such situations. I've had all sorts of women, and some men, come to me about that. Maybe others would be judgmental, but I've always found their stories are quite often very complicated, and slapping a negative judgment on them right off hardly does their story or them any justice. Perhaps what you're saying is that most people would think less of someone like that. Is that it?"

"Yes."

"Maybe a lot of people would, I'm not sure, but my pastoral instinct tells me Nancy won't react that way. Especially if I can talk with her."

"I don't think I can take that chance, Father."

"Well, what about this, then: may I at least bring up the subject to her?"

"How could you do that? Without breaking the seal of confession?"

"Precisely by citing confessional confidentiality."

"Do you think that will work?"

"I wouldn't have suggested it if I didn't."

"I'd have to think about that ... a lot, I'm afraid."

"You don't trust it?"

"Yeah," he said after a moment's reflection. "That's what I'm saying. I don't trust it." He paused again. "What if I were to call her anonymously and tell her that, more or less?"

"I think an anonymous call would result in her believing someone did actually murder her mom, and she'd bring the police in. And the complexities of that are enormous. If you had a little guilt the other night – which I hope you've been able to move beyond – I would just bet this scenario would leave you feeling like a fugitive. Don't go there."

"Okay. I'm just looking for possibilities I can live with."

"Keep working at it – that's okay. But that one isn't a good option. But back up. You were afraid you'd have to bring up your adoption. I don't think you'd have to. If I can convince you of that, would you then tell Nancy of your panic?"

"Maybe. But I can't see how to avoid the adoption if we talk. Tell me more."

"You can avoid it. You tell her about the quest you were on and all the war heroics you learned about. Show her the letter. And you don't need to go into anything else if you still don't want to. Just stop with the war stuff. Irene has her stroke. You panic. End of narrative."

"And if she's not satisfied with that? What if she doesn't believe it, or for any other reasons she feels she should talk to the police?"

"I'd be talking to her first. And I wouldn't connect the two of you unless I had reasonable assurances on that, Michael. Anyway, this is getting to sound like an attorney-client conversation before a plea bargain. I'm only discussing these things because you know there's something that has to be resolved, explained: why Irene's body was found at church. You're saying on the one hand that you're afraid of the consequences of resolving that, and on the other hand you're plagued by a nagging doubt or guilt ... or something like that. Do you want to resolve those feelings? Or not?"

Michael looked away from Father John. The light caught his profile and cast the look on his face in a peculiar fashion. It almost looked like he was in agony.

Father John pressed him. "Let me try. And I promise I won't bring you in on it."

Michael didn't look convinced.

"What can it hurt? I'll try not from the perspective that I know someone with inside information. Rather, I'll go at it from the angle of her own feelings, unresolved as they are so far."

Michael's face didn't betray anything. But when he spoke, he had moved off-center on the issue. "Okay. Try it. When will you do that?"

"I'll try tonight. It's not too late yet, I think. I hope."

"You want me to wait here?"

"No, for several reasons. You shouldn't get home too late and worry your mother. Anyway, you said you were going to tell her some things you learned from Irene. And, besides, I might not be able to reach Nancy right away."

"Okay. But will you call me if you learn anything?"

"Of course I will."

"I mean, tonight."

"If it's not too late, I will do that. Otherwise, I'll get you right after mass tomorrow morning. Okay?"

"Okay. And, Father … thanks again."

"I'll be in touch," Father John said, rising from his chair. He showed Michael to the door and turned immediately to go back to the phone.

CHAPTER XVII – THE SPIRIT

"It's Father Wintermann, Nancy." *Good. She's still up.* "I hope this isn't too late. I just have a small question about the report. Do you have it handy?"

"No, it's fine. I'm up. Let me get it," she said. "Here it is. What did you want to know?"

"Just to clarify: it doesn't mention any bruising, does it?"

"No. I checked for that. No bruises."

"Good to know that. Now to my question: does it classify the kind of stroke your mother had?"

"Pardon?"

"Was the stroke described in any way? Mild, or severe, or anything like that?"

"I don't recall. Let me check." She was silent for a few moments, obviously reading.

"Yes. Here it is. It says a couple of things. It describes it as a significant medical event. It also says the stroke was massive. Why? I mean, why would you ask? Is that important?"

"I think it might be, yes. It didn't occur to me to even think along those lines until I got a call from my parish in Algoma today. A long-time parishioner just had a stroke today and is in the hospital as a result. His was also a massive stroke, and the fear now is that he may not recover. But if he does, the further fear is that he may be in a vegetative state for the rest of his life."

"That's so sad."

"Yes, especially if you were to know the man. But that's not why I bring it up. Do you see the repercussions of that with regard to your mother?"

"I don't know what you're getting at, Father."

"Well, perhaps we should talk further about this, because it tells me that if the stroke had to happen, it was probably fortunate that it took your mother instantly the way it did."

"I suppose you're right, but I still don't understand … "

"What I'm getting at is this, Nancy – if you'll allow me to put it this way – it may not matter in the long run where your mother was found, after all. There was apparently no possible good outcome from this thing." *Is that insensitive?* He held his breath.

Nancy seemed flustered, unsure as to how to continue.

So Father John kept on. "Perhaps I'm not being very clear."

"Well, I don't know, Father. I … I think I need to think about what you just said."

"I hope this isn't another disturbing thought I've just piled onto a heap of others in your life right now, Nancy. If you want, take your time and get back to me tomorrow morning. We can talk after either of the masses. Oh, yes – I should have said that Father Bill's reinstated the earlier mass, and I'm to celebrate that one. We can talk after it, or else after the second one. And it doesn't have to be in person. It can be on the phone, if you can't come to mass."

"Tell you what, Father. I'll come to one of them, for sure. I want to pray for Mom. And then we can chat. But I must say – I'm still not sure what this means … why you brought it up. But I'll think about it. See you tomorrow, then. Sorry to rush off, but there are tons of things to do yet."

"I understand. Good luck with them. See you tomorrow."

He needed fresh air, he decided. So he went to the young man answering the phones that evening, the same one who had been there the past several nights. "I'm surprised you're still here."

"It's a little later than I usually stay, but I'm doing some homework, and I figured I might as well finish it here. And if other calls come, I can get them too."

"Good for you. I'll be outside walking for a while. If there are messages, please say I'll return shortly. Thanks."

He got his coat and stepped out into the cool evening air. He took a deep breath, then another. *Seems a little warmer. Or is it just my imagination?* Nonetheless, he found the fresh air bracing and set out, happily noting that almost all the sidewalks were clear of ice. He rounded the corner onto Bryn Mawr and decided to walk at least to the corner of California. The going was easy, so he kept on walking west, across California and on toward the park several blocks in the distance.

The ice was still clinging to tree limbs, and in the dark it looked as much like crystal as the first time he saw it Tuesday morning. In the daylight the sparkle had dulled, but at night the luster was restored – a trick of the artificial lighting, no doubt, but beautiful.

The urban scene, which was so different from what he was used to, had nonetheless a stark, even fierce, beauty, especially in the orange glow of the street lamps. His southern countryside, even the small-town streets, seemed warmer, softer in any light and any season. Here the angles seemed sharper, the colors colder. Maybe his subconscious predilections were asserting themselves, he couldn't be sure. But the contrast, while real enough to him, was nevertheless pleasing. He soaked up the frigid beauty of the scene as he continuing strolling toward the park.

Not only was nature in a physically frozen state, but the very scene before him seemed to his mind's eye to be frozen, as though caught in the split second of a strobe flash. It was like being handed a three-dimensional representation that could be twisted about and looked at from all angles, and you knew it wouldn't change all the while you viewed it. He found it somehow comforting. Unlike most everything else in the real world that shifted from second to second and thus defied easy scrutiny, this allowed for a long, slow and steady viewing. It set a very comforting tone to the moment, seeming to say that nothing was going to change soon – take your time – scrutinize if you wish, or reminisce, or just step back and look as long as you like.

That's what John Wintermann did. Walking slowly west along Bryn Mawr toward the park, he drank in the winterscape around him, and settling comfortably into its beauty, he slowly began to think about Irene and Michael and Nancy. The soft halos around the streetlights were multiplied hundreds of times over by the icy limbs and trees up and down the street. And he could picture the three faces amid the shimmering branches.

He suddenly realized that they were relatives. *Why hadn't I thought of that before? Strange! I wonder if Nancy will like that idea or not? Or, for that matter, will Michael? Perhaps that's something I should broach to one or both of them tomorrow.*

He continued walking, wondering what each of them would say to him in the morning, and he said a quick prayer to the Holy Spirit to guide their souls that night. How he wanted the two of them to like each other – no, to love each other. Love would resolve the thorny issues he and they were facing. Only love.

He reached the park and gazed deep into it for several minutes, enjoying the crystal beauty of the scene in front of him. And then he turned to retrace his steps. As he walked, he prayed and let his eyes soak in the beauty as he made his way through the crisp, almost brittle air. And he was refreshed but tired when he finally reached the rectory.

He ascended the stairs carefully. As he suspected, Bill's door was closed, so he continued as quietly as he could to his room. Sleep came easily and quickly, on the wings of angels, he was sure.

CHAPTER XVIII – PERSUASION

Father John was happy to see a good number of people at the early mass. Bill came over to make sure everything was set up properly and confided that attendance seemed back to normal. Father John celebrated mass slowly and deliberately, praying for Irene aloud and for Nancy and Michael in the quiet of his heart.

Afterward, the two priests shared coffee in the kitchen before Bill had to leave for the second mass. When Bill left, John went to check his suitcase, even though there was but a faint possibility he could wrap things up and leave later that day.

Bill had confirmed that Irene's funeral was set for Saturday afternoon, but Father John absolutely had to be on the road by then and would have to miss the funeral mass. He was hoping against hope that some clear resolution to the several loose ends dangling in front of him could be reached by then, but willy-nilly he was leaving for Algoma no later than noon.

He also remembered to call Algoma to confirm that a priest had been gotten for Saturday's confessions and evening mass. No matter what time he left tomorrow, he'd be cutting things too close to guarantee being present for them, and he almost certainly couldn't get away today. He waited 'til after nine o'clock and put the call through to the church secretary.

Sunday was Christmas Eve. He'd be able to handle that, of course, even though it would be busy, what with regular morning masses for the last Sunday of Advent plus Midnight Mass that night.

But his adrenaline would be pumping, and he'd be just fine, despite the previous day's long drive. Christmas was a wonderful time of the year.

Michael called just after he finished his Algoma call.

"No, I haven't heard further from Nancy, Michael. That's why I haven't called you yet."

"Nancy?"

"Irene's daughter."

"Oh, yes."

"Have you had any change of feelings overnight?"

"Well, first of all, I told Mom all about Dad's war record but nothing more. Not yet, anyway."

"Good. How'd she take that?"

"She was excited. She expects that I might even learn even more. I didn't comment on that."

"Okay. Anything else?"

"Yes. I'm leaning in the direction of talking face to face with Irene's daughter … Nancy, right?"

"Right. Nancy."

"And if I do, I'm pretty sure I'd like you there. Can that happen? Will you do that?"

"I already told you I would. And I'm still okay with it."

"Good. I suppose I'll just have to wait to hear from you, then."

"Right. And I'll call as soon as I know something. Can you come north pretty much any time today if – when – that might be needed?"

"I can, yes. But what do you mean *might be needed*?"

"That's assuming I'll judge it necessary and Nancy will be willing. But not to worry – I'll handle it. As to my question about being ready to come, you'll have to set out pretty much the moment I call because if Nancy's agreeable, we should strike while the iron's hot."

"I understand. And I can do that. Should I get ready now and stay by the phone?"

"Well, let's just say there's a possibility it will happen, and being ready will help."

"Okay."

"I'll be in touch, then. Bye, Michael." As Father John hung up, he hoped deep down that Michael wouldn't have to come for a face-to-face chat, but whatever Nancy wanted or needed was the driving force right now. *She should be contacting me soon. I'll wait 'til ten, and if she doesn't call by then, I'll give her a ring.*

She called barely ten minutes later.

"Father Wintermann?"

"Yes. I'm glad you called. Do you want to come over?

"I think that would be better. Is fifteen minutes okay?"

"It's good. I'll be expecting you."

When she arrived, Father John showed her into the little office. "Would you like some coffee?"

"Thanks. I'm fine. I've been thinking about what you asked last night, and I'm still puzzled why you brought that up. I guess I'm grateful Mom didn't have to look at years in some nursing home, but aside from that, I don't see the importance of that hypothetical possibility. It's all I can do just dealing with the real stuff right now."

"Well, I certainly don't want to grieve you further, Nancy, but there was a good reason why I brought it up. I think I mentioned it, at least briefly, last night."

Nancy looked puzzled. "I still don't understand, Father."

"If your mother survived that stroke, the probabilities wouldn't be good for her quality of life afterward."

"That I understand."

"I went on to suggest that it doesn't much matter where she was found. That is, it doesn't matter where she died."

"Are you suggesting that even if she didn't die outside church, that shouldn't be important to me?"

"Something like that, Nancy. Let me explain. I know someone who can shed some light on your mother's death, and I'm wondering if you want to talk with that person." He saw no way but to involve Michael.

"You mean there's someone who was with her or saw something, overheard something ... and you didn't tell me about that? Did you just learn that last night? Is that why you only brought it up then?" Nancy looked suddenly animated, perhaps upset. Father John wasn't sure.

"I heard a confession, Nancy. And you must realize I'm not at liberty to share that sort of thing without permission. I just received the go-ahead. The person involved would like to talk to you. That person has things to say about your mother and her death and about their connection as well. Do you want to speak with that person? I can arrange it – today, in fact."

"Why ever wouldn't I? Certainly I do. Did you doubt that?"

"Nancy, I've had to proceed very carefully. I've not been able to assume or presume much, if anything, about any of the parties involved. Please understand that. Now that I know you're interested, I can arrange for the three of us to talk as soon as possible. May I do that?"

"By all means, Father," she said, excited. Father John couldn't tell if, beyond being eager for the conversation, she was also angry, curious or something else entirely.

"I'll make the call. I think we can talk this morning. If I get permission, I may also be able to tell you more in just a few minutes. As I said, I have to be very circumspect. I'm dealing with the sacredness of confession here."

He stepped into the next room and called Michael, saying Nancy was eager to hear what he had to say about Irene. "What else may I say, Michael?"

"Like what, Father?"

"May I mention anything – generalities, to be sure – about your seeking your father's war information from Irene?"

"You can speak of that in general, I suppose. Will that make her more agreeable to talking with me?"

"It may well."

"Then go for it."

"I won't say anything about your being Irene's child – I don't know how to advise you on that. You'll have to decide for yourself as you talk to her."

"Okay."

"One last thing. Once again, her name is Nancy. Even so, I'll introduce you. May I use your full name or just your first?"

"I don't care."

"I'll use only your first name, then. You can decide if you want to tell her your last name. And I assume you still want me to be part of the conversation?"

"Yes, by all means. I think I need you there."

"All right, but I'll try not to say much. If you want me to speak to a specific point, you'll have to say so. Okay?"

"Okay. I'll get on my way now. This time of day, traffic shouldn't be bad. See you in forty-five minutes or so."

He rejoined Nancy. "I've changed my mind about that coffee, Father. May I have a cup? Or better still, do you have tea?"

"I'm sure we do. That sounds good to me as well. Let me ask someone to get us each a cup." He left for the receptionist, Mary Lou. When the tea appeared in several minutes, only then did Father John pick up the conversation.

"I received permission to tell you about the man who'll be here in little more than half an hour. He's in his forties, and he became acquainted with your mother because his father served with yours in Korea. As he tells it, your mom and he hit it off instantly. She was able to tell him a lot he didn't know about his father's stint in Korea. His dad hadn't been very forthcoming about his part in the war. But he did learn that his dad's sergeant was named O'Carroll, and that he was from Chicago. His dad died about two years ago, and since then he's spent a lot of time looking for that Mr. O'Carroll. He found your mother just recently, not knowing your dad was dead."

"I never heard anything from Dad about the war, either – or at least, not much. Who was this guy that served with Dad?"

"I'll let his son tell you, Nancy. Again, I'm not sure how much of that I may share. He'll be here soon. Is that all right with you?"

"Sure. I'm just excited, I guess."

The door opened and Mary Lou brought in a tray with two steaming cups of tea, honey and lemon. "Do either of you want cream?" she asked. They both declined, and Father John thanked her as she placed the tray on the desk.

After she had left, Father John served Nancy and poured honey into his own cup. They both sipped contentedly a few moments before Nancy broke the silence. "How long have you known this, Father?"

"Not long, Nancy. Only several days." Nancy didn't seem to realize that the time frame coincided with her mother's death.

"I wish I had known sooner."

Father John didn't comment, and Nancy didn't press him.

It was an awkward interval, waiting for Michael to arrive. There was only so much small talk that either could muster to fill in the time. Although, Father John did explain to Nancy that he'd have to miss the funeral. It helped that she understood.

Finally Michael arrived and was ushered into the office. Father John introduced him to Nancy.

The realization suddenly hit Father John that, since the two had the same mother, they were not only related, but they were brother and sister – half-brother and sister, really. *Why haven't I noticed this before?* He felt embarrassed. He also missed the look of surprise on Nancy's face when she first caught sight of Michael.

Michael began. "I'm so sorry you're having to bury your mother. I know how I felt when I lost Dad. But I can tell you something about her death that may help. At least, I hope it does. First, however, did Father John tell you how I met your mother?"

"Something about your father serving with Dad in Korea, I believe," she said distractedly, still looking strange. Neither of the men still seemed to notice her continued look of surprise. They certainly didn't react to it.

"Yes, that right, though maybe I should elaborate. I had searched for the sergeant O'Carroll my Dad knew in Korea ever since his death a couple of years ago. I finally found your mom the other day. We had a long talk, your mother even asking me to stay for soup. As we were talking, and pretty much about the time I decided to say goodbye, your mother suddenly fell forward in her living room and hit her head on the large Bible on her coffee table. You probably remember that she kept it there. I couldn't catch her before she fell – it was all so fast. When I got to her, she wasn't breathing and there was no pulse. I panicked, frankly. And I want to apologize to you for that. I didn't even think about CPR, and once I determined she really was dead, I decided not to call 911. Worse, I was embarrassed to be there when she died. I didn't know what it could have been. I thought she stumbled rising from her chair or something and I was afraid I would be blamed for her death. I now know it was a stroke, right? Anyway, in my confusion that night, I tried to think of a way to bail out of the situation." He was watching her face closely, but it was hard to read.

"I finally decided to place her outside church. I knew just enough about death to attempt being clever about all this. Rigor mortis would set in – when exactly, I wasn't sure, but I knew to keep her body in the same position it was in when she died." He paused. "I'm sorry to be so graphic, but I feel I should tell exactly what happened."

She nodded.

"I dressed your mother in her coat and waited 'til it got closer to the time for mass. But I hadn't banked on all that ice. I didn't even notice during that long night when it happened. But I managed to get your mom to church. I was hoping it would look like she was trying to go to mass. The ice, of course, was a huge complication, but by the time I had begun to move her, I couldn't back out of the plan. The ice not only made it difficult to maneuver her, but it would probably also make it hard to believe she'd venture out at all. But I was committed and I went through with it."

He took a short breath. "I certainly never meant to harm her, and didn't do anything to harm her. I would have helped her, but she died instantly. What I did was done to protect myself. I'm ashamed about that now, and sorry. I want to apologize for the grief I probably caused through this selfishness."

Finally he went silent. And Nancy seemed at a loss for words. And Father John sat silently, his face noncommittal. *So far, so good – but it all depends now on how Nancy reacts.*

When she finally spoke after an excruciating, long silence, what she said dashed Michael's hopes. "I can't believe this!"

The two men looked at each other, and Father John feared the worst. But to soften the blow that seemed about to fall, he asked: "Can't believe what, Nancy?"

Looking directly at Michael, she said: "You look just like my brother! He died in college, but given a little imagination to allow for his aging, I can see him there in you!"

Neither Michael nor Father John knew what to say, though Father John understood immediately how that might be the case. Michael was too befuddled to be able to think clearly and continued sitting in silence, confusion written all over his face.

"Well, perhaps, Nancy," Father John said, "but what about the things Michael just told you?"

She ignored the question and continued addressing Michael. "It's uncanny. If I didn't know he died years ago, you could be my brother."

Then it hit Michael, and he looked pleadingly at Father John.

CHAPTER XIX – REVELATION

The anguish in Michael's voice was palpable. "Nancy, please! I need to know if you can forgive me."

Nancy seemed to be looking more than listening. Michael's plea jolted her back into the discussion about her mother. "I'm sorry, Michael, but I'm having trouble getting over the shock. I do want to address what you've had to say. When Father John told me there was someone who 'knew something' about Mom's death, I was naturally interested. The more I thought about it, the more I began to wonder if that someone was present when she died. Then I began to worry that perhaps I was going to meet her killer. Pardon me for being blunt, but just as you felt the need to bare all, so must I."

She had fixed Michael with her gaze from the moment she first saw him. It was as if Father John weren't there. "But seeing your resemblance to my brother, I guess I subconsciously dismissed the possibility that you did anything to Mom. That's not rational, I suppose, but that's what was going on inside me. Now that I think through what you've said, I suppose I have a few questions and some comments."

Father John braced himself. He couldn't tell how Michael was reacting, other than that he'd looked tense ever since Nancy's first response to him.

"I guess I'm wondering why it's taken you three days to get around to talking to me. And I'm also wondering if you think what you did was a crime."

Michael measured his words and spoke slowly. "To tell you the truth, my first reaction was that what I'd done was a crime and a sin. In a way, there seemed little difference. The two were linked in my mind and in my feelings of guilt. I sought out Father John because my mother and I attended the funeral he had Monday, and I liked him right away. He's helped me work through the sin part, and he said that if I've committed a crime, I'd need to deal with that too, but later. First, he said, the sin. He helped me a lot, and I'm thankful to him." He glanced over at Father John gratefully, and Nancy followed his gaze. With that, Father John was in the conversation again.

"You should know that he was gently pushing me to settle things with you. So it seemed to me, anyway. He didn't force me. He allowed me to work through to that conclusion. And I wanted to do it, to talk with you – I wouldn't be here otherwise. It's important that you understand what happened Monday night and why ... and that you forgive me, if you can.

"As to moving your mother's body – whether that was a crime or not, I'm not sure. I suspect it was. But I don't really know. All I do know is that I didn't kill her – and that I panicked – and that I'm so very sorry."

"Father John obviously believes you, Michael, or he wouldn't have wanted this discussion," Nancy said. "I'm sure you understand my initial reluctance, however. After all, my mother is dead, and by your own admission, you were there. But I have to come back to that first shock of recognition when you walked in here. My brother died in college, but you could be his grown up twin. And that's pretty strong with me. I just can't see you doing anything to Mom."

She glanced briefly at Father John, who kept a noncommittal look on his face. "But moving the body! That still bothers me."

"Nancy, I told you I was afraid. Believe me, I wouldn't want to hurt Irene. You can't know how much I mean that!"

"Really? You only just met her several hours earlier. You expect me to believe that? That you *really* felt that strongly toward her?"

Michael looked helplessly at Father John for several seconds. It was long enough to become a plea for help, and Father John simply raised his eyebrows, as if to say *it's your call!*

Michael turned back to Nancy. "I truly felt that I couldn't take the chance of having the police come there. They'd have seen too much that I felt would be damning."

"Like what? Her body?"

"Yes, but also the letter she'd given me. Your father had written one to the Defense Department but never sent it. It had to do with the day he won all his medals in Korea. It was after a three or four day battle in which he helped hold a crucial hill against huge odds. A number of men were decorated that day, but not my father. And your dad felt badly about that. He went so far as to prepare that letter. But it didn't get sent. And your mother kept it all these years. The other night she gave it to me. And in my mind, the police would find that in my possession and use it against me when they found me with your mom's corpse."

"That doesn't make sense. I don't think the police would construe things that way."

"But I'm telling you, that's the way it seemed to me. And that fear took over."

He looked over at Father John. "Father, can you say it so it makes more sense?"

For the first time since he introduced them, Father John spoke. "I'm feeling so sad for you both right now. I'll try, Michael. But are you sure you want me to say more?"

Michael paused only a second before nodding yes.

"Well, then … here goes. Nancy, there's a very good reason why Michael reminds you of your brother. I'm sure it never occurred to either Michael or me that such a thing could happen before your shock at seeing him tonight. But, you see, Michael is related to you. He didn't know it before he met your mother." Father John glanced at Michael who had a look somewhere between fear and expectation on his face. "Irene was his mother too, you see."

Nancy's face spoke volumes about her total amazement.

"He learned that from Irene the other night. And while you should hear the whole story, the short of it is that she had Michael out of wedlock before she married your father. And Monday night, besides giving Michael that letter from your dad, she also gave him his birth certificate. That, perhaps more than anything else, was what Michael feared might be used against him, were the police to get involved."

He paused to let things sink in. "It's easy for anyone in hindsight to dismiss the frightful scenario Michael had conjured up. But I, for one, can see where fear may well have overcome him that night. Maybe you can, too, if you take a moment to think about it. But I said you should hear the whole story. And you need to hear that before rendering any kind of judgment about Michael or the other evening."

Turning to Michael, he asked: "Are you able to tell her, Michael?"

"I don't know, Father. Could you? Or could you at least begin?"

"Yes, I can, Michael. But please fill in where you're able."

Father John turned to look directly at a still bewildered Nancy. "It was, by your mother's own admission, Nancy, that against all odds she became infatuated with a man who would serve with her fiancé in Korea and then even more unbelievably would unwittingly adopt his own child after the war. When Michael showed up at her door, she believed he was there to blackmail her. No doubt, that wore heavily on Michael later that evening. If Irene could think that, perhaps the police could too."

Father John looked at Michael as if to ask *how am I doing?* Michael's unspoken look of acceptance encouraged him to continue.

"Your mother almost didn't let him in. She relaxed, however, when he didn't seem to know her secret, and she warmed to him as they talked. Over supper she made the decision to tell him everything. And by the end of their visit, she told him that in the short time she'd gotten to know him, she had come to love him very much."

He paused to look at Michael. "Would you say that's essentially it?"

Michael nodded affirmatively, his face a mixture of eagerness and sad remembrance.

Father John looked at Michael. "Michael can elaborate for you whenever you might want to hear the whole tale, Nancy. But for now," Father John paused to look at Michael, "do you want to briefly add anything, Michael?"

"Only, that as Father has told it, you may not have the sense of how wonderful that evening was for me, Nancy. I can't replace it, of course, but I also never thought I'd get the chance to experience the love of my real mother. I'm so incredibly happy that I did."

Nancy sat speechless, her face impossible to read.

CHAPTER XX – FAMILY

Michael looked at Nancy, fearing the worst. Even Father John was unsure how Nancy was taking this. After some moments of silence, Father John gently prodded her. "Nancy, Michael had a concern about telling you this because he feared that it might damage your mother's reputation in your eyes. I hope that hasn't happened here today."

Nancy finally spoke. "No, that's not it. It's just that I'm having trouble wrapping my mind around the fact that I have another brother. It's frankly something I've missed ever since Patrick died. Mom and Dad loved him, but he was the self-styled protector of his big sister, and I adored him. I've missed him terribly since that awful injury in college took him away. And now to find that I have another brother – and one that looks so much like Patrick – I just find it all so overwhelming. I need some time to get used to this. It's just an awful lot to come to grips with … " She lapsed into silence again, leaving the two men awkwardly adrift.

Father John cleared his throat quietly and waited, more or less content to allow Nancy whatever time she needed. Michael could barely contain himself, however. As Nancy sat twisting her hands in her lap, all he could see in her face were signs of a growing storm. He could contain himself no longer and blurted: "Nancy, I should never have come here today. I'm sorry to have put you through all this. You can't imagine … "

But Nancy cut him off. "No, Michael. You should have come. I'm glad you did. Don't you realize? You're the brother I've wanted for years now and never dreamed I could have."

"But your mother – our mother – wouldn't have died if I hadn't shown up. What awful timing!"

Father John spoke gently. "By now you should know better than that, Michael. This has reunited you with your own mother and it has helped you find a sister you never realized you had. It's a grace. Embrace it."

Nancy's suddenly calm eyes encouraged him from across the room. No longer content with the distance between them, she rose and went to Michael, taking his hands into hers. She gently pulled him up to stand beside her and then embraced him completely in an eloquent silence that Father John found incredibly moving. Michael broke into tears, and Nancy followed suit.

When at last they stepped apart, Nancy held his hands in hers and moved back an arm's length to survey him approvingly for a long moment. "Please don't ever regret coming here today, Michael," she gently pleaded. "I don't."

Father John cleared his throat again, this time a little louder. "There are still some things we need to be clear about. Is it indelicate of me to suggest doing that now?"

Nancy and Michael tore their eyes away from each other and looked at him, Michael sheepishly trying to blink away his tears. "Yes, certainly," he said, and looked back at Nancy with the beginnings of a grin coming onto his face. She grinned back, and they went to their respective chairs. But Michael thought better of that in mid-move and brought his chair next to his sister's. When he was seated, she took his hand, and they both turned to Father John, who was now obviously expected to move the conversation forward.

"It seems clear to me that Michael's fears have proven ill-founded, Nancy. Am I correct in saying that?"

"Oh, yes," she said with emotion.

"That means you needn't be afraid of the police either, Michael."

Before Michael could respond, Nancy said: "Oh, my God! The police! I'd forgotten. The desk sergeant that I contacted the other day – you remember, right?" she said, looking at Father John. "He left a message for me on my machine this morning. I haven't returned the call yet and didn't make much of it 'til just now. He may well want to pursue our conversation from the other day." She looked suddenly fearful.

Michael's look of puzzlement prompted Father John to explain briefly about Mr. Kwiatkowski. Then he turned to Nancy. "Don't get worked up. Whatever it is, we can handle it. Maybe he just wants to report back that officers did talk to your mother's neighbor."

"But what if he's talked to the policemen who were here at the parish? What if they've made him suspicious? After all, that's what I was thinking when I called him."

"Let's not leap to conclusions. You could call and find out, couldn't you?"

"Yes, but what do I say if he's come to those conclusions? I can't just tell him to ignore them. And I certainly wouldn't know how to share anything from our conversation here this morning."

Father John saw the cogency of her concerns. "Let's think a moment about this. I believe you do have to return his call. And before you do, there are some contingencies we need to think about."

Michael's troubled face told the priest he'd be of little help with that. But more to calm him than to enlist his aid, Father John said: "Feel free to put in your two cents' worth, Michael."

Then he asked Nancy: "Think back on your call to the precinct. Was it your impression that he understood your suspicions? Or was he merely reacting to your complaint about an unruly neighbor?"

"I honestly don't think he caught my real concerns at the time. But what if, as I said, he's talked to those two officers?"

"Well, that is a possibility, but doesn't the other scenario seem more plausible, that he's just getting back to you?"

"I guess so. But don't we have to be ready in case he has talked to those two cops?"

"Yes, you're right. We do. And I'm not sure yet how to handle that."

Michael finally spoke up. "Maybe the pastor here can help."

Father John was befuddled. "How?"

But Nancy understood immediately. "He may know the precinct captain," she said.

"So … ?" Father John said.

"So maybe he can put in a good word for us, if we need it," Nancy explained. Noting Father John's continued look of perplexity, she added: "This is Chicago, Father!"

"He can do that? Stop an investigation just like that?" Father John asked incredulously.

Nancy and Michael smiled at the same time. "Probably," they said simultaneously, as though they were explaining something to a child. "He can explain that I'm satisfied with everything, is the better way to put it. And it won't hurt if he knows someone in the department – which is an even-money bet," Nancy said.

Father John grinned. "Then let's go for it. Should we talk to Father Bill before you call?"

"I think that would be best," Nancy said.

"So how much of this conversation do we need to share with Father Bill?"

That question momentarily dampened the room's enthusiasm. Michael spoke first. "If need be, all of it, so far as I'm concerned."

"Well, you're certainly in charge, so far as confessional secrets go," Father John said. "Nancy, is that okay with you too?"

"No objections here."

"Then let me see if I can track him down," Father John said and rose from his chair.

Father Bill was soon being introduced to Michael and Nancy. Fifteen minutes later his genuine exuberance over the happy ending to Irene's death was a reassurance to the others. "I just happen to know the local captain. He went to grade school at St. Mel's with my younger brother. Want me here while you call the precinct, Nancy?"

"Why not, Bill?" Father John said, speaking for her. She nodded her approval.

Moments later the desk sergeant was speaking to Nancy.

"I wanted to tell you personally that I dispatched two officers to Mr. Kwiatkowski. I think he won't be troublesome in the future. But I also want to ask you something. Since your call, the two patrolmen who reported your mother's death have spoken to me. They're concerned about your mother being found outside church just after that horrible ice storm. They took pains to point out that they didn't write up the incident as suspicious, but they confided to me off the record that the incident didn't seem kosher."

"Thank you for sending the officers to my mother's neighbor, sergeant, and also for sharing the concern of the patrolmen who found my mother. But I am not worried about that matter now. My mother was a good Catholic ... "

"Yes, ma'am, but all the same, I think we're going to put this before the district attorney."

Father Bill had been standing next to Nancy overhearing the conversation. He tapped her on the shoulder and signaled that he'd like to speak.

"Sergeant, I'm actually calling you from St Hilary's rectory and I believe the pastor would like to speak with you. Just a moment, please."

She turned to hand the phone to Father Bill, but he said quietly to her, "On second thought, Nancy, I think I'll take this in the other room. Let me tell the sergeant that." He took the phone from her and asked the sergeant to hold while he transferred to another phone.

Nancy placed her phone on the cradle when she was sure Father Bill was on the line. She looked at the others quizzically. "Why'd he change his mind?"

Father John said, "I think he may want to spare us his arm-twisting. And, for all I know, he may have some personal things to say to the captain. I just hope he can get him on the phone now, that he's not busy with something else."

An awkward pause followed, but Father John got an idea. "Michael, why don't you and Nancy get better acquainted? I can use a bathroom break, anyway."

Their eyes lit up, and Father John stepped outside. Instead of heading for the restroom, however, he went to Bill's office, where he was on the phone with the police captain. He poked his head into the room and raised his eyebrows in a silent request to enter. Without breaking the rhythm of his conversation, Bill waved him in and indicated the chair in front of the desk.

As Father John sat down, he heard Bill saying: "Well, it's nice to hear your kids are doin' you proud, Jimmy. Actually, though, the reason I called has to do with the body that was found outside St. Hilary's last Tuesday morning."

He paused. "Oh, you heard about it, did you? It's nice to know you're still in the loop." He laughed. "Seems the officers who were here thought it odd she'd be out in all that ice." Another pause.

"Well, it struck me as odd, too, but apparently the guys didn't write it up as anything suspicious." There was a longer pause. Bill glanced at John and moved the index finger of his free hand clockwise in a circle, as if to say 'this is taking a while.'

"Yes, well I heard today from the lady's daughter. She says the desk sergeant – perhaps along with those two officers – wants to pursue the matter by placing it under the DA's nose."

He smiled at something the captain was saying. "Well, apparently they don't tell you everything, do they?" Bill held the receiver away from his ear so Father John could hear the captain's laughter. He grinned at Bill.

"Well, let me just tell you that the daughter is satisfied there was nothing amiss," Bill said. Another pause.

"That's right. She's not interested in pursuing the matter. I was hoping you could make sure that it ends there."

Bill was nodding as he listened, and then said: "Good. I'll tell her. And thanks. By the way, let me know when Jim junior graduates. Maybe I can make the ceremony. Law school's tough. The kid should get a few atta-boys when he completes it. Kiss Katy for me."

He hung up and looked at John. "I knew Jimmy would understand and could be relied on to take care of things. He's a great guy and a very good policeman. Doesn't hurt that he's Irish, either." He smiled and rose from behind the desk.

"You want to tell them, Bill?"

"No," Bill said. "You do that. Think I'm a fifth wheel in there. Besides, I've got things clamoring for my attention."

"Okay. But let me give you their thanks before you go get busy somewhere. I'm sure this will be a big load off both their minds."

"Don't mention it. What are pastors for, anyway?" He grinned and headed to the receptionist's office.

When Father John rejoined them, Nancy and Michael looked up anxiously at him. The thought crossed his mind to drag out the announcement, but he quickly decided otherwise. This was no time for games. "It's all set. Piece of cake! Father Bill seems pretty cozy with the precinct captain – calls him 'Jimmy'!"

Michael looked relieved. "Great. We're been making up for lost time in here. I just learned that the funeral's tomorrow. Nancy wants me sitting next to her."

Father John smiled. "Is the wake tonight, then?"

"Yes," Nancy said. "And Michael's coming to that as well. I think it's time I introduced him to his other family." Michael was smiling.

"Come to think of it," Father John said as he glanced at his watch, "I think I can make that too. I'm going to put off driving home 'til tomorrow. It gives the roads an extra day, just to be on the safe side." Nancy didn't seem to understand, so Michael explained about the long drive Father John would have and about his concern about icy roads.

"Oh, but they're okay, Father. I'm pretty sure."

"The city streets are, I know."

"The highways, too," Nancy said.

"Even so, I'm a bit drained from all this, and I'll give it 'til tomorrow morning. I can get away after mass and, with luck, will be home by midafternoon. In case I do need more time, there's a priest coming in for the evening mass. So I'm in good shape in that department. Where's the wake, Nancy, and what time is it?"

She told him, and he promised to be there. "With any luck, Father Bill will be going, and he surely knows the way." He smiled.

"Oh, he's coming, all right. He told me he was," Nancy reassured Father John.

"I best be on my way," Michael said, "so I can clean up and get back looking presentable." The other two said their goodbyes to him.

But Nancy hung back after Michael left. "I'd like to talk to you for just a minute more, Father."

"Sure."

"No need to go back into the office. I can say what I want to right here. I'm very grateful you wanted Michael to bare his soul to me."

"As Michael already said, I didn't push him into that."

"But it's clear to me you favored it."

Father John didn't respond.

"Michael and I talked about mom's 'reputation' while you and Father Bill were on the phone. He said again how worried he was that I'd see his revelations as tantamount to dragging her name through the mud. Couldn't have been farther from my mind! But I had to explain that and put his fears to rest.

"If I were younger I might have a more idealized idea of what people should be, a more romantic notion that my mom was the prettiest on the block, and things like that – that she couldn't possibly have a child like that. But when you get older, you realize life's a lot grayer than that. I don't hold that against Mom at all.

"To hear Michael repeat what she told him, Mom apparently kept her integrity pretty well intact once she realized she was pregnant. And all those intervening years she kept her love for her child alive, even against all the odds – kept it to herself besides. Pretty tough old lady, I'd say. And very loving! Just as I want to remember her!"

Father John was smiling gently. "Against all the odds, you say! That was her phrase to Michael several times. She didn't have a deep love for those odds – certainly not in the earlier years of her saga. But, you know, this was a case of looking odds right in the eye and besting them. I don't think you can explain that in any other terms than divine providence, Nancy. God had a hand in this – from start to finish."

"Right down to making sure you were here for Michael and me. Thanks."

Father John reached over and hugged her. *Couldn't have said it better myself. Thank you, Lord.*

He saw her to the door and went looking for Bill. The day was moving on apace. It was past two o'clock, and he thought it wouldn't be out of place to time for a cocktail before supper. *And this meal is definitely going to be my treat.* If they timed it right, they'd get to the wake and be back early enough for a nice, long night's rest.

CHAPTER XXI – CHRISTMAS

Father John was on the expressway and homeward bound well before midmorning. With a long ride ahead of him, he was determined to put the past week into perspective before thinking about the Christmas services awaiting him at St. Helena's.

He was convinced that the Holy Spirit had been at work in his life the past few days. That was a no-brainer. He'd been an unwitting pilgrim, a stranger surprised by grace. He had visited no fabled shrine, hadn't deliberately sought a holy relic. Yet he'd encountered a lover's bones – what are saints other than lovers? It was not the first time he'd been graced into lives needing spiritual patchwork, and he had no doubt it could happen again. Never had he sought these moments, always he'd rejoiced in them, and always he'd felt enrichment for himself as well as those he helped patch into wholeness.

These past few days he'd been a shepherd visited by angels and brought to a modern-day Bethlehem. As one of Jahweh's little folk, he'd witnessed a holy birth and stood in the providential presence of God at work in His world. Bethlehem, he knew, meant 'house of bread,' and this Bethlehem had given him spiritual nourishment. How apropos at Christmas! Gloria in excelsis Deo!

He promised prayers that love continue growing in the souls of Michael and Nancy and that Irene's strength take new life in them. At this very hour of her funeral, he offered the first of those prayers, giving thanks to God for turning death into loving life, for transforming his own delay into a facilitation of grace, for driving fear from timid hearts and for opening them to love's greater possibilities.

He'd been ministered to as well, of course. In a new place and climate, he'd been led to revelation. The trip turned out to be so much more than he thought he was taking on, but it had also proven to be what he'd predicted. There was people-patching, after all.

Now he was heading back to familiar territory and a different kind of Bethlehem, one where he'd not be such a stranger, though he'd still be one of God's little folk. He vowed to use the remaining hours of his trip preparing himself to stand in awe before the one birth that his faith told him gives meaning to all other births, physical and spiritual.

The thought struck him that he'd been the victim of something like that fabled Chinese curse: 'May you live in interesting times!' Maybe those long-desired mysteries were going to become standard fare. *No, this has surely been just coincidental!*

He settled back for several hours during which he could tweak his Christmas homily, when suddenly he became aware of traffic congestion ahead of him, and he braked to slide behind a pickup from Tennessee. *He's a long way from home!*

Then the vehicle's bumper sticker got his attention: IF YOU GET ANY CLOSER I'LL FLICK A BOOGER AT YOUR WINDSHIELD. He had to admit it. That was more outrageous than anything he'd seen around Algoma, and it helped ease him out of the alien world he was leaving and back into the more familiar one of his beloved Southern Illinois.

Merry Christmas, John! Won't it be nice to get back home!